THEIR ADDRESS WAS 43 WINDTHORNE ROAD, DANBURY, CONNECTICUT

Mari lived with her mother and father at 43 Windthorne Road. She was three years old when her mother, asleep in the next room, was brutally murdered. Since then, she has lived with her father and grandparents in her grandparents' house. As she looks forward to her senior year and beginning her life as an adult, she focuses on finding her mother's killer by looking for clues in her family's attic. She soon believes that the solution to the murder lies in the house where her mother was killed. Under the guise of visiting colleges, she enlists her best friends to take a road trip with her to visit the house where the murder took place. Who owns it now? What clues might they have? What clues might exist in the neighborhood? Mari is a determined young woman on a quest to find the person who killed her mother and will look wherever she can and try whatever is available to awaken her memory of that terrible day.

By Joanne Russo Insull

Picture Books

Dugan, the Dog Who Said, "Mom"

The Shoe by the Side of the Road and Other Missing Things

Asinella, the Nanny Donkey

Sarah and the Crows Clean Up

Don't Follow Pino!

Short Stories

How I Got My Dining Room Set

Help in the Time of Coronavirus

Marching for Peace

Where Do the Dead Go?

43 WINDTHORNE ROAD

Joanne Russo Insull

Cover art by Kelly Ann Artieri

ISBN 979-8-9850454-6-8 (paperback)
ISBN 979-8-985-0454-7-5 (ebook)

For my Great-Grandmother and the women in my life who have taught me strength and determination

Chapter 1

My mother was murdered in her sleep 14 years ago by someone with an ax. I was three years old and was sleeping in the next room. I'm seventeen now and I don't remember much about her; not her face, not her voice, not her touch, not her smell after working in the garden or after a shower. I have an album of pictures of her with her curly black hair. Sometimes she wore it up, sometimes in a ponytail. In my favorite photo she was dressed for some party–maybe New Year's Eve–in a sparkly black dress, her hair in a million curls, with a big smile and soft, happy eyes. Her name was Marianne Corelli Franklin; my parents named me "Mari" after her.

Since the murder, my father and I have lived with my grandparents in a farmhouse in Rochester, New York. There are woods behind the house where I used to play when I was little. I like to go to these woods to walk and think. I was surrounded by the smells of soil, rotting leaves and pine trees. Pine needles and pinecones crunched under my Chucks and pieces of leaves stuck to their white toes. It was a thinking day and although I was thinking about school, my friends, and choosing a college, my thoughts eventually turned to my mother. She has missed all the important moments in my life so far, and she and I will never get to share the rest of them, like picking out a prom dress, graduation, and maybe someday a wedding. I tried to pull memories of her out of my brain, but they just didn't come. Nobody knows who killed her, but I needed to know so the killer could be punished. Walking between the pine trees, I heard crows cawing overhead while I tried to figure out who did it. I did this a lot. I guess one could say I am obsessed with my mother's murder–not only who did it, but why. I didn't have many pieces to solve this puzzle, but I was determined to find them and put them together. Why now? What prompted this after 14 years? Graduating from high school and getting ready to leave home for college made me want to put this part of my life in order; to do something important for my mother by solving her murder. I wanted us both to have the peace of putting her to rest at last.

The night it happened I was in bed in our house in Connecticut. I wonder if the murderer came into my room. Was I supposed to have been killed too? I got goosebumps thinking of such a bad person in my house. I was trembling inside and out, and I couldn't catch my breath.

I didn't remember the house but there were a few pictures in my album. White with green shutters and a yellow door with the number 43 in brass. In the front was a flower garden and a maple tree with a baby swing hanging from the thickest branch. Attached to the house was the garage. In one picture, there was a green minivan in the driveway, perhaps waiting for my mother to drive to the store, go out to lunch with one of her friends or take me someplace. In the picture I saw houses next door and across the street. A nice neighborhood for a family.

My father never talked about my mother or what happened to her. When I asked about her, he would pick up a paper and pretend to read, or he'd get up from the table and clear the dishes. Sometimes he just left the room without making any eye contact. This had gone on ever since I was old enough to ask him about her; no answers, no response, no stories about her, no details about her murder. I stopped asking long ago, but I thought about her murder every day.

Within days after my mother was murdered, my father took us to Rochester, New York to live with my grandparents. We never returned to Connecticut; at least I haven't. Maybe my father went by himself, but I doubt it. Grandpa insisted that we leave Danbury and move to Rochester. I'm not sure why. Grandma and Grandpa are my dad's parents, and Grandma said Dad needed help because it was such a sad time and he needed someone to help take care of me.

My hair was black and curly, like my mother's. Grandma's hair was straight and the color of stainless steel. She wore it medium length, just to her jaw, and in a ponytail when she was working. Grandma still had a little of that "hippie" personality–she cooked from scratch, baked her own bread, had an organic garden where she grew a lot of veggies, and cut and chopped wood for the fires that she built in our fireplace. And she was strong! She built a brick fireplace in the backyard to bake bread. The oven was heated with the wood that she chopped herself from the trees she cut down in the woods behind the house.

She loved to go for walks in the woods in the morning. Regardless of the weather, she took off for an hour of what she called her "meditation time." She came back with pink cheeks and a sparkle in her eyes. I think the pink cheeks were from the frigid weather or the workout she got, but her sparkle probably came from her meditation. I must have inherited my love of the woods from her.

Grandma filled in for my mother at mother-daughter events at school. Even though she wasn't my mother, at least I got to go and have someone with me. She baked my birthday cakes, took care of me when I was sick and held me close when I cried and needed consolation–and she was the only one in my family willing to talk to me about my mother. She said, "You know, Mari, you do look so much like your mother. Just go look in the mirror to get a picture of what she looked like." She took me to the mirror and pointed out where I resembled her. She pointed not just to my hair, but my eyes. After she did that, whenever I looked in the mirror I smiled, trying to see my mother's smile in my reflection. When I asked her about my mother's death, Grandma got tears in her eyes and told me that all I needed to know is how much she loved me. Maybe that was enough for Grandma, but it wasn't enough for me. Asking my grandfather was a dead-end too, except for one day when we were alone, and I asked him about the murder.

Grandpa took off his glasses and ran his hands through his thinning gray hair. He said, "Mari, there's not much to know. Your parents were married right after college graduation and your father got a job in Danbury. After you were born, we wanted you near us, but it wasn't possible. When your mother died, I told your father it would be best to move to Rochester. There was a lot of publicity about your father and mother. Your father got lots of calls from reporters and lots of visits from police detectives trying to find the murderer. People who watch too much television and too many crime shows accused him of murdering her."

His eyes glinted with anger. I was mad, too and although I hated to think about it, I wondered if my dad had killed her. It seems like the police always suspect the husband when there's a murder. I didn't want to think of him that way, but it was happening in my head. Maybe that's why Dad never talked about her. Maybe his reaction when I asked about her colored my feelings about him. Maybe he was the guilty one.

"Your mother's murder was never solved," Grandpa said. It sounded to me like he was ready to end the conversation, but I wanted to keep it going because this type of talk was so rare.

"Who do you think did it, Grandpa?"

Silence. Since I got no answer, I changed the question.

"I wonder what happened to the house. Was it sold?"

"Yes. It took a while because of what happened there, but your father sold it at a bargain price. He just wanted to get rid of it."

"Who lives in it now? I asked.

"Not sure," said Grandpa. Then he walked away and picked up the current issue of *Finger Lakes Magazine* and headed off to his recliner. The conversation was over. It left me wondering who murdered my mother and who bought our house.

Chapter 2

The first weekend after school started, we had a science project as our homework assignment. On Saturday afternoon I got a text from my best friend, Emily.

"Project?"

"See you at 1:00."

Emily and her family lived across the street. I picked up my notebook and phone and walked over to Emily's house. We'd been friends since we were in preschool. She lived in our neighborhood with her mother, a teacher, and her father, a police officer, and an older brother, Seth, who was a freshman in college in Boston. He had a full college scholarship as well as soft, blue eyes, and wanted to be a writer when he graduated. He loved books and working with pre-school-aged kids and volunteered whenever he could to read books to the children who lived in the homeless shelter downtown. Did I mention how cute he was and how blue his eyes were? I was already missing him even though he'd left for college only two weeks ago.

Emily came to the door with her curly little dog, Max. Max's tail was wagging as he gave the growly bark that he always gave when he saw me. He liked to be on my lap. When I petted him and tangled my fingers in his curly coat, I totally relaxed. I had read about therapy dogs being used to help people who had been through tragedies, and based on how I felt when I held Max, I knew he helped me. Even though Max wasn't an official therapy dog, he was a natural!

We went upstairs to Emily's bedroom, and I sat on her bed with Max curled up next to me. Em sat at her desk ready to work. "Okay, Mari. The heart. What can we find? Start Googling 'heart' and let's see what comes up."

We took out a list of questions that our science teacher had assigned. Emily was into school stuff, maybe because her mother was a teacher. Whenever she had a question, even when we were little, her mother told her to "look it up" –and she did. Emily never let me take the easy way out on these projects. She made me look up stuff, too. Then when Google gave us a list of references, we needed to choose the best ones and find them.

"What would Seth tell us to do?" I thought, my mind on his blue eyes. The last time we did a project, he showed us how to choose references. I remembered what he showed us and followed his instructions.

"Em, this is going to be a great project," I said. "I'm glad we're working together. I hate group projects because a lot of the time I wind up doing the work and the other people take the easy way out. But not when I work with you. You work hard and you make me work."

"Somebody has to keep after you," she said. "Remember the time we were in math, and you fell asleep?"

I did remember. "You sat there and pinched my arm every time you saw my eyes start to close. I had bruises for a week after that."

"How many?" she asked. "Or is that too much math for you?"

We started laughing hard over that one. We always had a good time together. We had known each other so long that we knew lots of stupid things about each other, things that we could tease each other about. She teased me about the crush I have on her brother. She knew about my mother and although we didn't talk about it a lot, Em listened to me talk about her when I felt sad. When she had plans with her own mother, like lunch or a concert, she checked to see if they could include me.

"OK, Emily," I said. "All we need now is somebody to write these reports for us!" We laughed because we were both feeling good about finding the information we needed. She came over and bounced onto her bed with Max between us. We didn't need anyone to do our work for us because we were good at writing. We gave each other a high five, I picked up my notebook and phone, and then went home.

The four of us sat around the dinner table. Grandma had baked bread and made beef stew for dinner. Everything smelled great. I was starving after working on the project all afternoon and my family seemed to be in a good mood.

"Did you and Em get a lot done today?" Dad asked.

"We did. All the research is done for our project and all we need to do is write it. It was on the heart. The laptop made it easy to find information.".

Grandma chimed in, "When I went to college, we looked everything up in the card catalog in the library. The computers were huge and took up the whole room. They weren't used by students. We had to use real books."

"No, Grandma. That's impossible!"

Grandpa backed her up on this. They all began to laugh and joke about computers in the "good old days," as Grandpa called it.

"I think I might want to get a better laptop," I said. "A little stronger so I can do more things. Maybe I should get a job so I can earn some money to buy a new one."

"What would you do?" Dad asked. He didn't look happy.

"Babysitting might be the best idea because I can make my own hours."

"That sounds reasonable, Ed," Grandma said. "It sounds like Mari knows her own limits, and her own mind." Grandma was always good at providing backup.

The four of us cleaned up the kitchen, Grandma loaded the

dishwasher, and I went upstairs to my room to design a flyer to advertise myself as a babysitter. I distributed my information around the neighborhood and soon my phone was ringing.

My babysitting jobs were mostly for afternoons after school. After the kids got to know me, their parents asked me to babysit on a Friday or Saturday night. My father didn't want me to babysit past 11:00 pm, so it would take a longer time than I had hoped before I had enough money for my laptop.

I enjoyed babysitting for the Fernandez family. Their three-year-old daughter, Amelia, was an assertive little girl, telling me "No" about a hundred times an hour. She loved to play catch and peek-a-boo and I liked to watch her because she was about the same age I was when my mother died. Everything she did, playing, talking, feeding herself, even saying, "No" a hundred times an hour made me wonder if I did those things the same way. When her mother came home and picked her up and kissed her, I couldn't stop looking at them. It made me smile to think my mother probably did the same thing with me. I also felt sad to have missed those great moments with my mother, all because of a murderer.

One day Amelia's mother asked me to babysit and when I arrived, the TV was showing a video about their family. I wondered if my grandparents, or even my father, had any videos of us. Up to this point, all I had was the photo album with just a few pictures, but maybe somewhere in the house there were some videos that I could use to recreate my history with my mother the way Mrs. Fernandez had done with her family. It was time for me to step up my efforts to find anything available to fill in my mother's story.

That night at the dinner table, as we sat together, I asked my father and my grandparents if there were any videos of my mother in the house. Dad and Grandpa said they didn't know, but my grandmother promised to look in what she called her "video archives."

Grandma said, "There's a lot of stuff in the attic that came from the house in Connecticut. Everything is very dusty because it's been up there untouched for so many years. Maybe there are videos there that you could look for. I know there are more pictures packed away."

I headed to the attic to see how big the search would be. There were lots of boxes, but not enough light to search at nighttime. I decided to put it off until the weekend. This might be a big task, and I also needed time to get my college applications done.

Chapter 3

I had started looking at colleges, or at least their websites. I was sure that my father and grandparents had some firm opinions about where I should go, but I had decided that I wanted to apply to colleges in Connecticut.

"Mari, you can go almost anywhere. I'm not sure why you want to go to Connecticut," said Dad. "We really need to see a few places. We can look nearby, or we could look further downstate. I'll get some time off and we can take a road trip to look at some colleges, but I really don't want to take you to Connecticut."

I felt annoyed and snapped back at him, "Why, Dad? Is it because Mom was murdered there?"

As soon as I'd said it, I'd regretted it because of the looks on everyone's faces. I couldn't explain the specifics, but their jaws dropped, and their eyes were very wide open. I was upset and I wanted to get away from them quickly. I was angry at how protective they were, the way they wanted to keep me from anything having to do with my life before we moved here. What were they afraid of? Did they know something about my mother's murder that they didn't want me to know? What did they think I'd find out if I went to Connecticut? Lots of questions needed answers, and I needed to find the truth. I ran to my room and slammed the door, threw myself on the bed, and picked up my phone to call Emily. Before I had started the call, there was a knock on the bedroom door. I knew Grandma would be the one who would come to find me and try to calm me down.

"Mari, I know you're upset, but your father doesn't want you to go to Connecticut. There was just too much horror there."

"Grandma, if that's how he feels, he should come and talk to me himself. I need to hear it directly from him, and I need to know why. She was my mother, and I think I have the right to know more about her, particularly about how she died and who killed her." I could feel my eyes brimming with tears, but the anger I felt wouldn't let them run down my cheeks.

I've never seen you this way, Mari."

"What way?" I asked. Those were my feelings and she had no right to question them.

"You've always been a quiet girl, but now I'm seeing so much anger. I'm wondering how this happened so suddenly."

"You shouldn't have to wonder, Grandma. I've lived without my mother for most of my life because of a murderer, and nobody did anything to solve the murder— to find who killed her. If you were in my shoes, you'd be full of anger too. I feel like I'm about to explode! And I want to go to Connecticut because I believe that that's where her spirit lives and she won't rest until somebody solves her murder."

Grandma came over and sat next to me on the bed. She put her arms around me and said, "I understand, Mari, and my heart breaks for you. I'm so, so sorry you are going through this." I had never seen my grandmother look so sad, and I believed her words and the concern in her voice.

"Just remember that your father is angry, too. He doesn't express it, but don't forget that he found your mother's body covered in blood. It was horrible for him. He loved your mother very much, and he loves you too, even though he doesn't show it much or in the way you think he should. But this has damaged him."

It was then that my tears came, along with deep sobs. Grandma held me tightly while she told me it was good to let those emotions out. She stayed with me for a while, and I lay down on the bed exhausted. She rubbed my back until I fell into a very sound sleep.

During that sleep, I had a very vivid dream about my mother. She was standing in front of our house in Danbury, pushing me in the little swing that hung in the tree in the front yard. Everything was in color. I saw the bright greens of the grass and leaves on the trees, I heard the chirping of the birds, saw the blue sky, the white of the house contrasting with the dark green shutters, the yellow door on the front of the house, the shiny brass number 43 on the door and my mother's black hair and beautiful smile. She was smiling at me, and I was laughing with every push. Then somebody walked up the driveway and my mother's smile disappeared, and an ominous look came into her eyes.

I woke up feeling very frightened and a little disoriented. It took a minute or two to get my bearings, then I sat in bed for a few minutes just going over that dream in my head. Was my mother trying to send me a message? Maybe she was trying to tell me who her murderer was. I got up and went to take a shower and as I stood there letting the warm water wash away the salt of last night's tears, I decided that I needed to go to Connecticut to find out more about what happened.

I came down to breakfast to find that Dad had already left for an early meeting at work. Grandpa was working in the garden, but Grandma was sitting at the kitchen table having coffee.

"How are you feeling, Mari?" she asked. "Did you sleep well?"

"Sort of." I said. "I had some strange dreams."

"Excellent dreams or awful dreams?" she asked, just as she had asked me many mornings before when I'd told her I'd had a dream.

"Both," I said, as I ate my breakfast. "Thanks for listening to me last night."

"Anytime you need to talk, I'm here," she said with a gentle smile.

I picked up my backpack and my phone, kissed her goodbye

and left for school. Emily was leaving her house at the same time, and we usually walked together.

"Mari, you look awful today. What's going on?"

"Thanks for the compliment," I said, feeling annoyed. "I had a rough night."

"Did you have a fight with your dad?'

"Em, something's not right. Grandma and I had a talk last night, and she told me how much my dad loved my mom, but I'm not sure. He never talks about her; he has nothing that belonged to her in the house. He doesn't even have a wedding picture or a picture of the three of us together. It's as if he doesn't want any reminders of her at all."

Emily had a big frown on her face. It was the same face she made when she worked on a hard math problem.

"Maybe he's still grieving, and it's just too sad for him," she said.

"I'm not so sure. He seems so angry at everything, especially me, I think. Like I said, something's not right."

Chapter 4

My eighteenth birthday was coming up. We usually went out to dinner to celebrate, and the birthday person got to choose where the four of us would go. I loved Italian food, so I picked a small Italian restaurant owned by a young couple from Rome. White linen tablecloths and napkins, candles and flowers were on the table. My favorite dish was lasagna, and theirs was the best. The bread was crusty on the outside and soft on the inside, and the dessert tray was full of awesome choices. The background music was Italian classical, soft, and relaxing. The food was great, and the waiter brought me two cannoli for dessert with a candle stuck in each one. I thought it was a suitable place to celebrate becoming an adult.

"Buon compleanno," the waiter said, which meant "Happy Birthday" in Italian.

That was what I liked about this restaurant. Even when it wasn't my birthday, I felt special when I went there. As we ate dessert and drank our espresso, Grandma and Grandpa gave me a beautiful package, and when I opened it, it turned out to be a laptop. At last!

"Oh wow," I said, "Thanks so much. This makes me so happy!"

"You're welcome, Mari. Use it to write those science reports." In my mind I was planning to use it to find out more about the college in Danbury and my mother's murder.

I got up and kissed them both. Even the waiter was smiling.

Then Dad took a small box out of his jacket pocket. The box was wrapped in gold printed paper with a small white bow. When I opened it, there was a gold locket inside. When I opened the locket, there was a picture on each side. One picture of Dad, and one of Mom. My Mom! I could hardly believe it! There was a small card in a gold envelope. I opened the envelope and read the card.

"Happy birthday, Mari. Love, Mom and Dad."

I looked at my dad, and he had the hint of a smile on his face. His eyes softened.

"From Mom," I asked?

"It belonged to her. It also belonged to her mother and grandmother before her, and after you were born, she talked about passing it on to you. She wore it every day, and she was wearing it the day she died."

OMG! This was hard to wrap my head around. Maybe it would seem creepy to other people, but to me it was so important. I couldn't take my eyes off the beautiful gold locket in my hand. It was heart-shaped, with flowers engraved on the front, and it hung on a gold chain. Engraved on it were some letters, XLIII. I asked Dad to help me with the clasp, and as soon as it touched my skin, I felt a warmth spread over my shoulders and face. Dad rested his hands on my shoulders after he fastened the chain. It was as if both my mother and father were giving me an enormous hug.

"Thanks so much, Dad. This really means a lot to me. It makes me feel like I have Mom with me. What do the letters mean?"

Dad told me the engraving was Roman number 43, but he was not sure what it meant. He was sure that she wanted me to have it because she'd told him when I was a baby, she planned to give it to me on my eighteenth birthday. Weird that the engraving was the same as our house number.

Dad hugged me and said, "I wish she was here with you more than you know."

I looked at his face, and he had a strange, far-away look. I'm not sure, but it was almost as if he felt guilty that my mother wasn't there. That night, I was in a deep sleep. I didn't remember any dreams, but when I woke up, it seemed as if I was in the same spot in my bed as I had been when I fell asleep. Maybe it was the locket that helped me sleep so well.

The next day I went to Emily's house to show her my mother's locket and to tell her about the birthday dinner. She loved the locket and thought it was the perfect gift for my birthday.

"What does the number mean?" she asked.

"My Dad didn't know, but it's the same number as our house address even though it was probably older than the house. It belonged to my other grandmother and my great-grandmother."

"Why do you think he waited until now to give it to you?" she asked.

"Because that's when my mom planned to give it to me–on my eighteenth birthday."

Emily had a serious look on her face. "Have you ever wondered if your dad killed your mom?"

I couldn't look at her. I had to look away so she wouldn't see the guilty look on my face. "Why would I think that?"

"I don't want to get you upset, but the other night I was watching a murder mystery about a woman who was murdered, and the police detective said, 'Let's look at the husband as a suspect. Nine out of ten times it's the husband.'"

I couldn't admit to her that I had thought of it more than once.

"I think your dad is very weird. Sometimes he scares me."

"What do you mean, he scares you?" I asked. "Why?"

"I don't know. He always has a serious face. He never smiles. And he's so strict with you all the time. When I go to your house, he never says hello. He just ignores me most of the time. I feel like I need to tiptoe around him because I'm afraid he'll explode or burst into flames. You've got to notice it."

"Sure. He's not the most warm and fuzzy dad, but I think it's because of what he's gone through."

"Or what he's done," she said.

Had she hit the nail on the head? Did my father do it?

"I just don't want to talk about it, Emily. Let's go out."

I needed to shut her down right now. I was pretty upset and a trip to the mall seemed like an excellent idea to clear my head. Dad gave me some money for my birthday, and I wanted to shop for some new shoes. Hopefully, the mall and the shoe shopping will be a distraction for me. The bright lights, the endless stores and the smell of coffee, popcorn and those soft pretzels always made me feel better. I was hoping they'd be a distraction for Emily, too.

Chapter 5

Walking through the mall, we ran into Jodi and Nicole. Although Emily was my best friend, these girls were the next best. The four of us found seats at the coffee shop in a quiet part of the mall and ordered coffee topped with whipped cream and chocolate (our favorite). Jodi was our friend throughout high school and Nicole had moved here two years ago. Together, the four of us were a solid group.

My friends were my version of superheroes, only they wore regular clothes. What I liked most about each of them was how strong they were. Nobody would dare bully them. Once a group of boys ganged up on us. Every day when we walked home from school, they pushed us around and threw our books in the mud.

One day, the four of us, led by Jodi, saw them coming. We split up and cut through a backyard. When we came out on the other side, Jodi and Nicole came up behind the boys and knocked them down. Em and I took their books and threw them in the mud and told them that the entire school would find out how four girls had taken them down, so they'd better leave us alone. The bullying stopped, and the boys took a different route home. So much teamwork!

Each of my friends had something important that they brought to the group and to me. They knew the total story about my mother's murder and how nobody seemed to want to find her killer. They knew how important it was to me to solve the murder. These friends backed me up and are the group I'd go to when I needed somebody to listen. Em was the serious one. She was the most like me. I think that was the reason we got along so well. Jodi was the most assertive. Most of the time she'd say whatever came into her mind, and sometimes the rest of us just wanted to hide when she said it. She'd always know when she said something that should have had a filter on it, but then she'd get a look of mischief on her face and a twinkle in her eye and say it anyway. Most of the time Nicole and Emily and I couldn't believe some stuff Jodi would say, and our mouths hung open in surprise. We didn't want to be around her if she was angry. She could take somebody down with one icy look and a quick, sharp reply.

Jodi wasn't sure what she wanted to do in college or after, but I could see her as a teacher. Em and I told her that the kids in her classes would sit still because she missed nothing and knew all the tricks. She could also speak Spanish. Her family was originally from Mexico and although her English is perfect, she would speak Spanish with her family at home, especially when her grandmother, her abuela, was around.

I think Nicole was the prettiest of the four of us. She knew it, but she never made an enormous deal about her looks, except she was very particular about her long wavy hair and her eyebrows. I'm not sure how she kept them looking so nice. Wax? Tweezing? Threading? Whatever she used, it worked. She also loved to read; we all do, but she loved psychological novels with a lot of twists, like *The Girl on the Train.* She liked books by Jonathan Kellerman, a psychologist. She loved mysteries and was the quiet one of our group. She watched and listened carefully before she added her opinion.

We talked as we had our coffees.

"Mari just had an interesting birthday," Emily told them.

"Did you meet the love of your life?" Jodi asked.

"Right, Jodi," I said sarcastically.

I must have sounded more sarcastic than usual because Nicole sensed that something was wrong and asked, "What happened, Mari? It seems serious."

Emily then filled in the story.

"Mari and her father and grandparents went out to dinner, and her father gave her a gold locket that belonged to her mother. She got emotional about it and her family did, too."

"How emotional? What kind of emotional?" asked Jodi. "Sad, happy, angry? Mari, your family is so uptight. Your father is like a tightly wound-up spring. Was there yelling? Crying? Laughing? Nothing would surprise me."

"I was just very touched," I told them in a soft voice. I reached up to my neck, found the chain and took out the locket to show them. "The locket was from my mother, too, not just from my dad. But it was his idea to sign the card from both of them. It was her grandmother's locket. Her grandmother passed it down to her and now she has passed it down to me. It has an engraving on the back, some Roman numbers, XLIII." As I told my friends what had happened, I felt my eyes fill up. "The touching thing was that my mother was wearing it the day she was murdered. Because of that, I feel like it has her spirit attached to it."

"OMG Mari. It's so beautiful," said Nicole. "And what do the Roman numbers mean? If it's antique, they've probably got an important meaning."

"I know it's Roman Number 43, but I don't know what the number meant to my grandmother or my mother.

"I wonder if it's haunted," said Jodi.

"That's so dumb, Jodi," said Emily. "Jewelry doesn't get haunted."

But they agreed that it was a way for my mother to be close to me, and I needed to use it just for that purpose. That was why I loved my friends–they understood.

"I want to find out who killed her," I told them. "But I need to go to Connecticut to do it, I think. I want to go to Danbury so I can spend time there, see the house where she was murdered and learn how this happened."

"Have you been there?" asked Nicole.

"Never. Or at least not since I was little."

"Well," Jodi said in her own impulsive way. "It sounds like it's time for a road trip!"

The next day the four of us got together at lunchtime. Because Nicole was the most organized, she kept track of everyone's college applications, the colleges, and the deadlines for submitting them.

"Okay everybody. Did you finish your applications?" she said with an authoritarian note in her voice.

"We did," said Jodi. "And what about you?"

"Done!" replied Nicole. "Next, my parents are taking me on a road trip to see some colleges. We're driving to Massachusetts and stopping at four colleges along the way."

"You know what would be perfect?" Jodi asked. "What if we had a road trip— just the four of us? We could stop at our colleges so we could see everybody's schools. We could stop in Danbury so Mari could look around, not just at the college, but around Danbury to see where her parents lived, where she was born and where her mother died. We could tell our parents we were narrowing our list before we went with them."

That was a brilliant idea, and Jodi was on the mark with that one.

"Well," said Jodi, "this could go either way. It might relieve our parents if we save them from the endless college road trip like other families, or they could lock us in our bedrooms so we can't go."

A perfect Jodi-type response! We agreed to try convincing our parents and just in case Jodi was right, we needed to check alternate escape routes from our bedrooms.

When I got home, I went to my room to think. I held my mother's locket in my hand so tightly that after a few moments it was warm. I felt its energy move up my arm and into my chest, surrounding my heart. I knew it had to be a message from my mother to tell me she loved me, but I also believed that she was filling me with determination and strength. I knew she wanted her murderer found and brought to justice, and that determination would help me find that horrible person. First, I needed to take on my father and convince him I needed to go to Connecticut.

Just then, I heard Grandma call me for supper. I went down to the dining room. It was quiet around the table. I didn't feel like talking, but Grandma wanted to get a conversation going.

"What did you do today, Mari?" she asked.

"Em and I went to the mall to buy shoes," I said. "I got some strappy sandals and new running shoes. We also talked a little about where we want to go to college."

"Are you still thinking about applying to schools in Connecticut?"

"Yes," I said, quietly.

I stared down at my plate. But then I gathered my strength, and I looked at my family one at a time and I said with a firm voice, "I'm going to Connecticut, and I've picked out a college in Danbury that sounds interesting. I want you to help me do this, but if you won't help, I'll do it myself."

"Danbury?" said Grandpa. "Why Danbury? Or shouldn't I ask that question?"

He glanced over at Grandma as if he were looking for permission.

"Dad, let me handle this," said my father as he put his hand on Grandpa's arm. "Mari, you can't let this go, can you? You want to go to see the house where your mother died, don't you?" There was a touch of anger in his voice.

"How can I let it go? Nobody seems to care about finding her murderer at all. Dad, it isn't Mom's 'death' that's influencing this choice. It's her murder. We all should call it what it is."

My father put his head in his hands, covering his face. Grandpa crossed his arms and looked down at the table. I could feel the cloud of anger and desperation hanging over the dinner table like a thick fog. Grandma was quiet as she watched me take a stand for how I wanted to live my life, or at least the next four years of it. I thought I saw a glimpse of a smile flicker across her lips. At that point, even though there was still food on our plates, dinner was done, and I went to my room to work on my college applications.

I completed three applications that night on my new laptop. Not just the college in Danbury, but also two colleges in nearby Waterbury and New Haven. Tomorrow, I planned to go to the bank with my babysitting money to open a checking account and get a debit card for myself so I could pay the application fees, and then I'd find a part-time job to earn money for college. Babysitting would not give me enough money to do what I wanted. Whether or not I had my family's support, I would be in Connecticut soon.

Chapter 6

The application for the debit card was easier than I thought. Now all I needed was to get permission to go on the road trip with my friends. I knew that the four of us needed to come up with a solid plan, so we got together after school to put one together. We picked Columbus Day weekend because it was a long weekend, and it would be Fall—lots of pretty leaves and not much chance of snow. Our plan was to look at three schools between Rochester and Danbury, leaving time in Danbury to look around. The college list included Geneva to see Hobart-William Smith, the State University at Albany, and finally Western Connecticut State University in Danbury. The plan was to look around each campus and move on, without the usual tours and interviews. But when we got to Danbury, we'd do a little exploring unrelated to the college. Emily came up with a list of things we needed to do.

"We need to find places to stay between Rochester and Danbury. If we leave on Friday, we'll need a place to stay on Friday, Saturday, and Sunday. Then we can come back on Monday. Any suggestions?"

"A hotel might be nice, or a Bed and Breakfast," suggested Nicole. She would have loved to include a day at the spa, too!

We took out our phones and looked up the prices of hotels in Geneva, Albany, and Danbury, but the room rates, even for just one night, were too much. I told them I didn't have the money to do that. Neither did they. "Maybe we could go camping."

Nicole said she wasn't going camping. "It probably will be cold, and we'll need to take showers and wash our hair. How do we do that?" So, no camping.

Emily asked the group, "Does anyone have any relatives we could stay with?"

Jodi had an aunt and uncle in Albany who she visited every few months. "I'll call them and ask if they can put us up." She had them on speed dial. Her aunt was eager to welcome her and the other three of us. She took the phone aside to talk longer with her aunt, and when she finished talking, she reported that her aunt and uncle would be glad to host us.

"OK," I said. "There's one place. That could be Saturday night. Now we need Friday and Sunday. Let's work on it and get back together tomorrow for more planning. We have two enormous questions. First, how will we get our parents to let us go, and second, where can we get a car?"

I got discouraged, but I knew my friends, and I knew we could pull this together. That night I told my family about the "college" trip. But before dinner I held my locket in my hand and talked to my mother.

"Mom, please help me do this! I need to find the person who took you away from me, and this is the only way I know how."

And then I went down to dinner. My grandparents and dad were waiting for me to join them.

Grandma started off the conversation as usual. "How was school today, Mari?"

"It was good, Grandma." I sat down and stopped for a minute while I thought about what I would say. "I need to tell you what my friends and I are hoping to do over Columbus Day weekend."

I could feel the locket resting just above my heart, which was beating so loud I thought for sure everyone could hear it.

"What is it, Mari?" said Dad, buttering a slice of homemade bread.

"We want to look around three college campuses, Hobart and William Smith, State University at Albany, and (my heartbeat raced even faster) Western Connecticut State University. Four of us are going—me, Emily, Jodi, and Nicole. We're still making plans. But we'll need a car, and we'll need a place to stay on Friday night and Sunday night. Do you know anyone we could stay with in Geneva and Danbury? Jodi's aunt said we could stay with them at their house in Albany on Saturday."

Dad's face twitched. He didn't look happy. Anger flickered across his eyes. I put my hand at my throat to feel the locket, and Dad's expression changed; he looked resigned.

"Look Mari. You know how I feel about your playing Nancy Drew and going to Danbury. At this point, something's telling me I'm fighting an uphill battle with you. So, here's what I'll do. I'll pay for hotel rooms for you and your friends for those two nights because I want you in a safe place. I'll even make the reservations for you. But I want to check with Jodi's parents to make sure that her aunt is okay with these arrangements."

Wow! I never expected that, but I needed to push my luck a little further. "Oh, and Dad," I said. "Could you get a room big enough for the four of us—like maybe two king-size beds–so we can all stay together?"

As he got up from the table and walked toward the living room, I heard him say, "Sure." I couldn't believe this. It wasn't Grandma who convinced him, it was me, and wearing Mom's locket gave me the courage and the words I needed. The way I saw it, Mom was with me and she wanted her murderer found. I texted my friends with the news. Now all we needed was a car. Emily asked her father if we could use his car. He drove a new SUV with plenty of room for the four of us. She said he was thinking it over. I hated that! I hated waiting to find out what parents decided. A lot of times they'd tell us they needed to think it over, but what they meant was they were thinking about how to tell us "No" without looking bad. I wished I had a car, but there was no way on the money I made from babysitting that I'd ever be able to buy one, and since my dad was paying for the hotel and didn't want me to go anyway, I didn't think he'd lend us his car, too.

Em's dad finished "thinking it over" and decided he couldn't spare his car that weekend. Now what?

I went to my bedroom to do some homework that I needed to do before our trip, and after a while, Grandma came upstairs. She sat on the bed and said, "Mari, I know you and your friends really want to do this. But most important to me, it's something very important to you. I'll lend you my car for the weekend. But I need you to promise me you'll drive carefully and put your phones away while you're driving. I also want you to call in every night, so we know you're okay."

I couldn't believe what I heard! Grandma did this for me and for my mother. I jumped up and gave her an enormous hug.

"Thanks so much, Grandma. We'll be careful, I promise."

I was about ready to cry because I was so happy. Grandma gave me one of her smiles and left the room. I could hardly wait to text everyone and let them know. We agreed to meet the next day at school to plan our trip.

I don't think I slept much that night. My mind was racing. I wasn't planning the trip to the colleges but thinking past that to finding information about my mother's murder. Where would I go? Who would I talk to? I made a mental list of where I needed to go and who I needed to see. We didn't have a lot of time in Danbury, so I needed to plan to be efficient. Tomorrow I'd go to the internet and see what I could find and start from there.

I finally fell asleep and had a dream about my house again. I saw it. 43 Windthorne Road. White with green shutters. The bright yellow door. Mom pushing me in my swing that hung from the tree in front. And then the hooded figure appeared again in the driveway and walked toward the yellow door. Was it a man? I couldn't tell. The figure walked in slow motion. As it got to the front steps, I woke up. I was sweating and scared. But now I had a plan to find out who the person was. I was trembling as I held my breath and I said to the figure, "I'm coming to get you. You won't get away with what you did." And I meant it.

Grandma and I had breakfast together, and she asked me how the planning was going for our trip. "Mari," she said, "I want you to be very careful. This could be dangerous for you, and I want you to use your head. Please, please promise me you won't do anything that puts you at risk! If anything happens to you, I'd be beside myself with grief and it would break what little spirit your father has left. This is a very strong warning, Mari, I mean it. I'm lending you my car and I expect you to be careful and responsible and don't take any chances."

I had never heard my grandmother speak so strongly and with such fear. "Grandma," I asked her, "Why are you so scared? Do you know something about the murder that you're not telling me?"

"I've told you before that I don't really know anything except how brutal it was. If I knew who did it, I would have told the police just to have the person arrested. I'm worried more about you four girls going on such a lengthy trip by yourselves to a strange place where you don't know anybody. I know you feel you've got to go, but I don't think you'll find out anything new. If the police couldn't figure it out, I don't think you will, either."

"But I need to try, Grandma. I know I'm taking a risk, but it's an important risk. And if I don't do it, who will?"

I got up from the table and put my arms around her.

"I promise I'll be careful. I'll be okay."

"Mari, you're smart. Be sure you're using your head in this. That's all I'll say."

Chapter 7

The four of us got together at lunchtime in the cafeteria and made a list of things we needed to do to get ready for the trip. Gas, snacks for the car, warm jackets, hats, and gloves just in case it got cold. Sometimes October gets freezing in Upstate New York and probably in Connecticut. Boots in case there was mud. Money for food and "incidentals." Grandma's car had a GPS so we could get there and find our way around. We also needed a list of addresses for the GPS. And of course, our phones and chargers. We divided up the list of things to do and the list of places we would visit.

I had my list and most of it had to do with getting more background information about my mother and what had happened when she died. Places to go in Danbury, people to talk to. So that afternoon during my free period, I went to the library to start my research. I found a computer and piled my books around me so people would think I was in the middle of a project. I needed to concentrate. I entered my mother's name into the search engine. "Marianne Corelli Franklin" I typed. Up came a list of entries.

I scrolled down the list to get an idea of what was in there and found my parents' engagement announcement in the local paper, followed by their wedding picture and a description of the wedding. She was a beautiful bride, and they looked so happy! How could my friends act suspicious? My father never would have killed her!

Then I came across what I was looking for–an article in the Danbury paper about her murder. The article was fifteen years old and read, "Danbury Woman Brutally Murdered." I sent the file to myself so I could keep it on my laptop and read it later. About every five years there was an update, another long rehash of my mother's murder, the days before it and the days after. I forwarded those articles too. Now I needed to get back to class. Later, I'd look for more information.

I wanted someone to talk to about what was happening. I didn't feel that I could go to my father or grandfather about my thoughts about the murder, and although Grandma was sympathetic and helping me, I knew how she felt about my pursuing this, and her opinion was not what I was looking for. My friends, especially Emily, were great. Emily was the best listener, but I needed something more, and I didn't want anybody to judge my thoughts or what I wanted to do. If my mother were alive, I'd talk to her. And then a thought came to me–a brilliant one!

I could talk to my mother, or rather I could write to her and let her know how I was feeling and how my search was going. Not that I believed that she would answer me, but writing to her would help me think and sort things out. When I got home, I looked in my closet and found a journal that Emily had given me last Christmas. I finally found something to use it for! I sat down, opened the first page, and wrote.

Dear Mom,
I miss you.

And then I poured out everything that had happened onto that page and the next four pages. When I finished, I signed it, "Love, Mari." Now I felt fantastic, relaxed, and full of energy at the same time. I felt clean, like I just got out of a hot, soapy shower. I was ready for this.

Chapter 8

The Friday of Columbus Day weekend was Superintendent's Day in our school district, so we had the day off. This gave my friends and me the chance to leave early. Grandma had invited everyone for breakfast before we left, pancakes and bacon with enormous glasses of orange juice. We packed up Grandma's car with backpacks, suitcases and food and left around ten o'clock after a hug for everyone from Grandma.

"Be careful girls and stay in touch."

"We will, Grandma," I said, closing the hatchback door. We all got in and I started the car.

"The adventure begins." said Emily, "Or I guess I should say Mari's adventure!"

Soon we were heading for Geneva to visit Hobart-William Smith College. From Rochester, the drive was about forty-five minutes along the New York State Thruway. Geneva was a small city, typical for Upstate New York, sitting on the shore of Seneca Lake, one of the Finger Lakes. The colleges were a combination of two colleges on the same campus, Hobart for men and William Smith for women, although now they had combined into one co-ed school.

It was beautiful. The buildings were mostly stone, although there were a few constructed of brick, and a few large old homes housed the fraternities. Located in the center of Geneva, across from the lake, it descended a hill and then rose to the top of the next one. It reminded me of Hogwarts, not just old but full of tradition.

We toured the campus with a student, a sophomore from Illinois, then we went to lunch in the dining hall where we spoke to some other students about life on campus. Nicole liked Hobart-William Smith because it was small and had a New England feel to it. Em and Jodi agreed that it was nice, but there was not much to do in Geneva except at the college. They'd have to drive to Syracuse or Rochester for any excitement. We stayed there most of the afternoon. Nicole took some information and pictures, then we drove down the road to a large hotel on the lake and checked in. Dad did an expert job making the reservation because we had a suite with two king-size beds. The windows looked over the huge, beautiful lake, and at that moment the sun was setting. We ordered a pizza from the local pizzeria, a little place near the college. It tasted so good to me, which I think was because I was with my best friends and on my way to find out more about my mother's death.

I took out my journal. Em said, "Isn't that the journal I bought you, Mari? Looks like you're finally using it."

"Yeah," I said. "I needed to write to clear my brain. I'm glad you gave it to me because it's perfect for what I'm doing."

"And what is that?" said Emily as she tried to peer over my shoulder to see what I was writing.

I slid my hand over the page so Em couldn't see what I had written. "I'm writing to my mother every day. I need to talk to her, and this is the only way I can see to do it."

Emily looked at me with sadness in her eyes. She put her hand on my shoulder and said, "I'm tired so I'm going to bed. I knew you'd find some excellent use for the journal. I'll see you in the morning."

Jodi and Nicole went to bed too, while I went to the desk and wrote to my mom to tell her about my day. I told her how Grandma and Dad provided what we needed--pancakes, a car and room reservations, and I told her about my friends who were helping me do this. They sure knew how to support my effort. And I told her about my best friend Emily and how she knew me so well and how great it was to have her as my best friend. I wondered who her best friend was. Didn't everyone have one? I signed the day's entry, *"Love, Mari,"* turned out the light and went to sleep.

It was a deep sleep with a familiar dream. There was our house, white with dark green shutters and a yellow door, the shiny brass number 43. Me, sitting in the swing hanging from the tree in the front yard, my mom pushing me. And then someone in a hoodie walking up the driveway toward the house, this time walking past my mother and me toward the front door. The figure turned toward us, but I still could not identify who it was. The figure climbed up the four front steps toward the door. A hand reached for the shiny brass doorknob and just as it was about to touch it, I woke up, sweaty and breathless. I had had another nightmare. I got up as quietly as I could without turning on the light so I wouldn't wake up my roommates, went to the bathroom for a drink of water, and felt my way back to bed. After deciding that I needed to write the dream down and share it with my mom tomorrow, I pulled the covers up over my shoulder and fell back asleep.

We slept a little late, and even though it was October, the sun was out when we woke up. We showered, dressed, packed, and went down to breakfast in the hotel dining room.

"How did everybody sleep?" asked Jodi.

Nicole said she would have slept better if Jodi hadn't snored. Jodi said that Nicole tried to take up the whole king-size bed. In our bed, Emily didn't move all night. She didn't complain at all about me, either. But I knew better. I knew I must have disturbed her when I got up, but she didn't say a word about it.

After breakfast we went for a walk along the lake. It was so pretty! Fall leaves and sun glinted off the water. We took lots of pictures and agreed that this was a very tempting location for college, but we needed to move on. We checked it off our list, packed up the car and got back on the Thruway.

Our next stop was Albany to visit the State University branch there. As we drove, we talked about what we wanted in college.

"I have to admit that my mind isn't on college itself," I said.

"We know," said Jodi. "You're a woman on a quest!"

"Not funny, Jodi," I said. "Right now, finding my mother's murderer is the most important thing in my life."

Taking a hint, Nicole changed the subject. Halloween was coming, and she suggested that we talk about the scariest thing that ever happened to us. I asked if she meant scary, like being in a haunted house at Halloween or a real-life scary experience. Nicole said we should leave it up to the person sharing, but regular Halloween tales were kind of boring and she'd like to hear real-life stories.

"OK Jodi, you start," said Emily.

Jodi sat quietly for a few minutes, which was very unusual for her. I knew that she was thinking, but I also knew her well enough to know that she was looking for something safe to share, something we wouldn't make fun of or brush off. Although she had a great sense of humor and loved to tease the people around her, she found it a little hard to take when the roles were reversed.

"I'll pass," she said. I guess sharing was a little too scary for her right then. I knew eventually she'd come around.

Nicole stepped in.

"You remember that my family moved here two years ago because they offered my father a job? We all liked Ohio where we lived, but there was no opportunity for him there. My mother had an excellent job in Columbus, but she gave it up and agreed to go because Dad's new boss said that as part of the new job agreement, they'd have a job for Mom too. My parents asked my brother and me what we thought about the move. I really didn't want to go. I told them about a hundred times and tried to convince them to change their minds. My brother was only 5 years old, so he didn't really care. But I was in high school! I had friends! I must have cried myself asleep every night for weeks! We had to pack things away to straighten up the house so we could sell it. I needed to throw away or donate a lot of my stuff. I still can't find my favorite blue sweater."

She sounded like she was going to cry.

"Every Sunday was an open house that the realtor set up. I hated that strangers were walking through my room and opening my closet and looking at my personal stuff. I thought that maybe if nobody bought the house then we couldn't go."

Emily asked, "Were you more scared about leaving Ohio or coming here?"

Nicole paused for a few minutes to think. "Both," she said, "but coming here to a new house, a new school in a place where I'd have no friends was the scariest. It was a long, boring drive, seven hours, and I think I cried the whole way. I already missed my best friend Olivia so much! And it scared me to start school because I was sure there'd be bullies or mean girls waiting for me."

Emily turned to look at her sitting in the back seat and asked, "Were there?"

"No," said Nicole. "Just you guys." And when she said that we all laughed. "You were nice to me that first day at school and it made me feel so good. I wasn't scared after that."

"Glad to be of service!" I said. "You're lucky we were in an excellent mood that day."

At that point the GPS said, "You have reached your destination." We were at Jodi's aunt and uncle's house. I called my grandma to let her know that we had arrived in Albany.

"How's it going, Mari?" she said.

"It's good, Grandma. We're all ok, and we're having a wonderful time. We got excellent information at Hobart and William Smith, and we'll see the State University at Albany this afternoon. We just got to Jodi's aunt's house, and she's cooking a big dinner for us. I think Mexican food."

"That sounds great, dear. I'll let your dad know that you're in Albany."

"Oh, and Grandma, tell Dad the rooms in Geneva were good.

Tell him we all say thanks. The breakfast was delicious, too."

"Ok, Mari. Take care and drive safely."

Jodi's aunt was a warm, friendly woman named Elena, with a big smile and a hug for each of us. Although we had never met her before, she welcomed us as if we were a part of her family and told us to call her "Aunt Elena." Jodi's family had come here from Mexico, and they loved their traditions. Jodi spoke fluent Spanish with Aunt Elena when we first got there but then quickly switched to English.

We could smell Mexican food cooking, and Aunt Elena showed us our rooms, which had beds covered with colorful handmade quilts. The walls of the bedrooms were decorated with framed art posters. I saw the name of Frida Kahlo on the poster in the room I was sleeping in, a poster of the artist sleeping, and I remembered from art class that Frida Kahlo was from Mexico. It was a great poster for a bedroom. Aunt Elena asked us what our schedule was, and we told her we were going to the college this afternoon for a recruiting meeting which included food, and we'd be back by 5:30.

She said, "OK girls, we'll see you then. Dinner is at six o'clock and we're having tortillas. Don't eat too many snacks!"

Compared to what we had seen in Geneva, the university was a unique environment. It was a vast campus with lots of buildings, much larger than the small, upstate college we had just visited. All the buildings had lots of floors and seemed huge. There were classrooms that held five hundred students, an enormous library and performing arts center and separate buildings for many of the departments. We had a tour given by a student from Brooklyn who covered a lot more ground than the tour we had before. I knew this was not the college for me, not just because of the size of the campus, but because I wanted to be in Danbury. After a visit to the dining hall for some New York State snacks (apples, cheese, and apple cider), we gathered some brochures, took a selfie in front of the sign, and headed for the car, which wasn't easy to find in the giant lot, but I used the horn button on the remote that Grandma used when she couldn't find it. The horn went off, the lights turned on, we found the car and the four of us got in. We were not that far from Aunt Elena's house, and I swore we could smell those tortillas cooking.

When we arrived back at the house, it was nearly six o'clock. Aunt Elena's husband, Uncle Mike, had returned from work. Jodi introduced us to him, and Uncle Mike was as warm as Aunt Elena was in welcoming us to their home. We helped Aunt Elena set the table and make a salad, and then we all sat down to dinner.

Uncle Mike asked about the campuses we had visited. He had been to the Albany campus often and knew it well because he was an electrician who had helped to do some wiring upgrades in the buildings.

"Are any of you interested in coming here for school? I hope Jodi is," he said with a smile. "It would be nice to have her nearby."

We all looked at each other, and although we didn't want to disappoint him, we each said in our own way, "We just haven't decided yet. We still need to go to Danbury."

"Why Danbury?" he asked, becoming serious.

Jodi said, "Mari wants to go there, and she has an important reason."

She turned toward me with an embarrassed look. "Maybe I shouldn't have opened my mouth right now. Mari, I'm sorry."

"That's okay Jodi." I turned to him and explained, "Somebody murdered my mom when I was three years old, and they never found the killer. It happened in Danbury, and I want to find out who did it since nobody seems to care."

Uncle Mike looked shocked. His jaw dropped open. "What? This is horrible! I'm so sorry. This sounds dangerous. Hey, this isn't your job, Mari. It's not up to you. The police need to do this. Didn't they have any suspects back then?"

"Not any except my father."

Uncle Mike got quiet. He glanced from me to Jodi. Then Emily looked up slowly and said, "That's what I think, too. I think it was her father. Whenever a woman is murdered, lots of times it's her husband or boyfriend. I don't think Mari needs to look in Danbury. She doesn't need to look far at all."

I was feeling betrayed at what Emily had said, and I picked up my plate and took it to the kitchen. I stood at the sink and cried. Aunt Elena came in and put her arms around me.

"You poor thing," she said softly. "I'm sure that this weighs heavily on your heart. You're putting a lot of responsibility on yourself, not to mention that you're putting yourself in danger. My heart goes out to you, but please, you need to be careful. Please make sure you talk to the police before you do anything on your own."

I sank into Aunt Elena's hug. It felt so comforting to me to have someone reach out to me that way. I promised her I'd be careful, even though I wasn't sure how to do that. I'd just have to see how things unfolded in Danbury.

"You seem tired," she said. "Why don't you go to bed a little early? You've been driving all day and you must be exhausted. You've got a bit of a drive tomorrow too, and you need the rest. Leave the dishes. Mike and the others will help me."

I didn't want to leave that warm hug, but I went up to the bedroom and took out my journal. I held onto the locket around my neck as I made the day's entry. I could feel the engraved "43" on the outside, and I ran my thumb over it as I wrote in my journal.

> *"Dear Mom,*
>
> *Jodi's aunt was so kind to me today. She gave me a feeling of being cared for, which I need right now. She told me to be careful. You need to show me what I need to be careful of because I'm not sure.*
>
> *I miss you. Love, Mari."*

I lay on the bed looking at the picture of Frida Kahlo. I remembered another picture of her from art class with her dark eyes and even darker eyebrows. She had such a powerful face, and a determined look. She looked like a strong woman. I made a mental note to look her up on my laptop, then I turned out the light and fell asleep.

The next morning, I woke up to find Emily sitting on the side of the bed.

"Mari, I'm sorry if I upset you. I really didn't mean it. We just have different ideas about who did this to your mother."

"I know, Em, but I need you to stop accusing my father. If you really think he did it, then why did you come on this trip?"

Em said, "I wanted to be supportive, that's all, and maybe it isn't him."

"You're making me mad. I'll find out the truth myself, and then we'll see, but for now, let it go."

"OK, I'll stop. I'm sorry I hurt you." She put her hand on my shoulder to console me. I got up and gathered my clothes for the day and went to take my shower.

Aunt Elena made us a big Mexican breakfast with huevos rancheros, ham, and homemade cornbread. We could hardly move afterward. She also packed a lunch of sandwiches on rolls, apples, and fresh cut-up veggies. She was so kind to us, and especially to me.

"Thank you so much for everything, Aunt Elena." I was practically in tears because I appreciated her caring so much. Uncle Mike was standing nearby. Each of us gave them a hug. We got in the car, reset the GPS, and I drove toward Connecticut.

Chapter 9

Danbury was about two hours from Albany. We talked about Aunt Elena and Uncle Mike as we drove.

"They're like having another set of parents," Jodi said, "They're here for me when I need them."

I knew what she was talking about. Aunt Elena, this woman who was a stranger to me just twenty-four hours ago, who welcomed us into her home and consoled me when I was so upset, comforted me, and treated me like her own family. We all agreed that staying with them was a special experience. Both Uncle Mike and Aunt Elena provided us with food, were welcoming and showed real concern for us.

Em suggested we go back to talking about our scariest moments. Jodi picked up the conversation.

"My scariest moment came more than once. You've heard me and my parents speaking Spanish, right?"

As if we were a chorus, the three of us said, "Si`" Jodi chuckled and began to tell us her story.

"One time we were on the highway near the Canadian border, and we stopped to do some shopping. We were speaking Spanish, and some woman gave us a hard time. She asked to see our IDs, and my parents refused and told her she had no right to ask for them. She called the police, and the ICE officers came all dressed in camo uniforms and had guns. I'm sure you've heard about them. They control immigration. They demanded to see our IDs. I know my dad was mad, but he told me later it wouldn't have been good to get angry with the ICE people, and it might even make things worse. I was so scared. I was afraid that they'd take us away. Maybe they'd even deport us, even though we're citizens. What would we do if they locked us up? My parents stayed calm and answered their questions, and finally they let us go."

"You must have been pretty relieved that you got away from ICE," Nicole said.

"We were, but we knew it could happen again. It happens here because we are close to the Canadian border. I need to tell you, it scared me. We know people from our church who they deported to Mexico."

"Yeah, but they can't send you there if you're a citizen, right?"

"Right, but if you aren't, they could take you away."

Nicole asked, "Then why don't they just become citizens?"

"It's not that easy. It's not cheap, and it takes time."

"I hate to say it, Jodi, but maybe you shouldn't speak Spanish in public," said Nicole.

"There's no reason to stop." she said, her eyes flashing. "Spanish is our language too."

She was right. There was no reason for her family to stop speaking Spanish. It made us angry that they had to deal with what they ran into. It was awful how that run-in with ICE scared her and her family. If I thought I might be taken away and sent to another country, I'd be terrified. Not only that, but the woman who called the police needed to mind her own business.

Chapter 10

The Fall leaves were deep red and orange. The temperature had dropped a little, and it was feeling cold. When we stopped for a break and got out of the car, we could smell the leaves and the smoke from the wood-burning fireplaces in the houses nearby. In Upstate New York in the fall, there is always the smell of apples in the air, too, and it was Fall. At one point we passed a field with two deer grazing. They looked up, and we caught their attention for a moment. They froze and then turned to run off, flashing their white tails. There were some fleece throws in the back seat of the car, and my two friends in the back seat snuggled together under a red plaid one, while Emily, sitting in the front passenger seat, wrapped herself in a dark blue striped one. I cranked up the heat in the car.

We didn't have far to go after that break, just an hour and a half to Danbury. Everyone got quiet, like it was naptime. I think they fell asleep. The quiet was good because it gave me a chance to think. I thought about the stories Nicole and Jodi told us about being afraid. Nobody enjoys being afraid, and I tried to imagine being in their place and being afraid; like Nicole's fear of moving to New York or Jodi's fear that they would take away her family. Of course, I thought about my mother. Had someone been planning to murder her and did she know it in advance? She must have been terrified if she saw her murderer coming toward her. I wondered if she knew the person. They found her in bed, so maybe she was asleep when he…wait a minute! I said, "he" but could it have been a woman? Could a woman have done something so brutal? Would she have the strength to do it? My heart was beating loud and fast as I thought about this possibility. My eyes widened, as if I was trying to see. I wondered if the police ever looked at that possibility.

Everybody woke up, which was good because we were crossing into Connecticut. Danbury was right over the New York/Connecticut border, and a big blue sign welcomed us to the state. Shortly after, we pulled into the hotel parking lot. I sat in the car for a few minutes while my friends got out and collected their stuff. Emily leaned back into the front seat and looked directly into my face.

"Are you ok, Mari? You look pale. Was the driving too much?"

"No," I said. "I'm good. Let me get my stuff and we can eat lunch. I'm just hungry, I think."

We checked in and after we brought our stuff to our rooms, we went to Jodi and Nicole's room and broke out the lunch that Aunt Elena had made for us. There was guacamole, my favorite, and I licked every bit off my fingers, which made Nicole cringe.

"That was very classy," said Nicole.

"I really couldn't help it. It was so good. Can we stop at their house on the way back?" I said, laughing. "Your Aunt Elena is the best cook, Jodi."

Now that I knew Aunt Elena, I wanted to see her again. I didn't want anything to happen to her, and even though I had known her for such a brief time, she was important to me, and I didn't want to lose her. If she was speaking Spanish, would somebody call ICE again? I was glad they were citizens, but that didn't guarantee that they wouldn't be hassled.

Chapter 11

I wanted to see my parents' house, 43 Windthorne Road, but I wanted to go alone. Near the hotel was a big mall, and Em, Jodi and Nicole asked me to drop them off. I'd have time to go over to the house by myself and scope out the neighborhood. The mall was on the way, and we agreed to meet in two hours at the mall after they shopped, and I snooped.

The house looked the same as it looked in the pictures I had, except it seemed a lot smaller. It looked as if no one was home. There was no car in the driveway. Maybe the people were away for the weekend. I took out my phone and took some pictures of the house and the neighborhood. I walked up and down the street and as I walked back to my car, I noticed a guy driving an SUV who pulled into the driveway of the house next door. He was about my age, tall, with dark brown hair, and as he came toward me, he smiled.

"Are you lost?" he said.

"No. I used to live here a long time ago, and I wanted to come and see the old neighborhood."

"Which house was yours?" he asked.

"This one, number 43."

"I've lived here my entire life," he said. "What's your name?"

"Mari. Mari Franklin."

He sat on the front steps and invited me to sit next to him.

"Franklin? My parents knew your family."

"They did? My mother died here when I was a baby."

"Yeah, I heard about that. Pretty awful. Where do you live now?" he asked.

"Rochester, New York. My dad and I live with my grandparents. What's your name?" I asked him.

"Jake Henderson. You came all the way to Danbury just to see where you lived when you were a baby?"

"Well, kind of. I came with my friends to look at colleges along the way, and I want to look at Western Connecticut State. I want to go there so I can be in Danbury for school, but also because I want to do some detective work."

The curtains in the front window of the house across the street moved. I thought, "Somebody's nosey."

Just then another car pulled into the driveway.

"Hey, my mom is home from work."

She got out of the car and came toward us.

"Hi Jake," she said.

"Hi Mom."

"Do I know you?" she said, turning to me with a quizzical look. "You look very familiar."

Jake introduced us and told her I used to live next door, and then her eyes got huge.

"Oh my gosh, you are Marianne's daughter! Mari, my name is Brenda. The last time I saw you, you were three years old, but now, wow! You look just like your mother! That's why I thought you looked so familiar. The same black curls, the same eyes, and the locket."

"You recognize my locket?" I asked, reaching for the heart that rested at the base of my throat.

"Sure! Your mother wore it all the time. I used to tease her about the number 43 on it. I told her I knew that since it was her address, she wore the locket so that if she got lost, the police could bring her home. She laughed every time I said it. I sure miss her. We had a lot of fun together. You and Jake were born the same year and we went for walks, pushing our strollers around the neighborhood. Come here and let me give you a hug!"

She put her arms around me and held me. It felt so good to meet someone who knew my mother. I closed my eyes and smiled. Jake and I followed her into the house, and we went right to the kitchen.

"Sit down. I'll make us some tea."

We sat at the kitchen table next to the window. I could feel the sun on my shoulders warming me–or was the warmth of my feelings from being with Jake and with Brenda, this woman who was a connecting thread to my mother? She served green tea and brought out a bowl of nuts and dried fruit. A healthy choice, I thought, wondering if my mother would have been like her in serving green tea and a healthy snack. Maybe…

Jake teased his mother about her healthy choices, her snacks, her yoga classes. He was so cute, with his dark hair and brown eyes. He was wearing jeans and a shirt with his high school logo on it. I wanted to talk to Jake some more, but spending time with Brenda was limited and talking to her about my mother was a priority. Although my focus was on that, I needed to get back in time to pick up my friends. I told Jake and Brenda I'd be in Danbury with my three friends for the long weekend.

"I wonder if I could spend more time visiting you while I'm here?" I asked.

Brenda said, "Why don't you and your friends have dinner with us tonight? After dinner, Jake could take them back to the hotel and you and I can talk."

Jake said, "Sure, there's a concert tonight at the college. Maybe they'd like to go. I'm meeting some friends there."

"Let me text them," I said. I had barely pressed "send" when the response came back, a big "thumbs up" and a collection of smiley emojis. "We're on," I said.

"Good," Brenda said. "Come over as soon as you can. I'll make something easy for dinner so you can eat right away, and they can get over to the concert with plenty of time to park. Jake, can you make sure they have tickets?"

"Yeah, Mom. They can buy them at the door, no problem."

Chapter 12

My friends and I decided to go to the hotel and change and then go back to Brenda's house for dinner. It was getting dark when I picked them up at the mall. They were full of questions.

"Who is this guy?"

"What was the neighborhood like?"

"What was this guy's mom like?"

"Do you think it's safe for us to go there?"

"What's for dinner?"

It was hard to hear the questions! Everyone was talking at the same time. As I answered them, we all started laughing. Then I had a question for them.

"Did you get anything good at the mall?"

"Nothing we couldn't get at our mall back home," said Nicole.

We started laughing even harder. When we got back to the hotel, I told them they had fifteen minutes to change, and then I was leaving for Brenda's house. I knew they'd never be ready in fifteen minutes, but I wanted to get back there soon, so I pressured them. It was more like a half hour before everyone was ready to get back in the car.

"Fifteen minutes?" I said as they piled into the SUV. And we all started laughing again. We drove to Windthorne Road and Em pointed out number 43. "Wow, Mari, there's your house.

It feels crazy to see it after I heard you talk about it for such a long time. Did it feel weird to you to see it?"

"It did. It looks just like the pictures I have, except there's no swing hanging from the tree in the front yard. It also looks a lot smaller."

I wondered who lived there now and decided that this would be close to the top of the list of questions I had for Brenda. Once again, I saw the curtains move in the window of the house across the street.

Jake introduced himself to my friends, and I saw Nicole look over at me from the corner of her eyes and raise her eyebrows as if to ask if I was interested in him. To be honest, I'd have to say that this wasn't where my mind was going. He was interesting, but I needed to focus.

The house smelled like my favorite Italian restaurant. Brenda had an enormous pot of sauce on the stove, and I could smell garlic bread in the oven. She welcomed everyone.

"Brenda, this is Emily. She's been my best friend since we were little. These girls know about my mother, but Em knows the most. She's been with me through the tough times, and she stayed by my side, just like she's doing this weekend. I couldn't have come here without her."

Emily smirked and said, "I sound like your emotional support animal."

Jodi and Nicole started in, still in the silly mood we had in the car. Jodi said, "So Em, if you were any kind of emotional support animal, what would you be? Maybe a koala bear? Or a goldendoodle?"

Nicole chimed in. "Maybe a monkey? Wait, I've got it, a platypus!"

We all started laughing, although Jake looked at us like we were crazy, and he wasn't sure if he should laugh or not.

"You see what kind of relationship the four of us have," I said to Brenda and Jake. Brenda was laughing, too. "Don't forget, we've been cooped up in a car for two days."

"I'm a little jealous," Brenda said. "Your mother and I had fun times together, too. You're lucky to have such wonderful friends. I'm glad to have met them and I think your mother would like them, too. It's good to have you all here. Now, let's eat!"

Brenda covered the dining room table with a red tablecloth, and red napkins rested at the side of our plates. She told us she used that tablecloth when she made Italian food so nobody could feel bad about getting sauce on it. That made sense to me, and I decided at that moment that I really liked Brenda. She had a sense of humor that leaned toward silliness for sure. Maybe my mother was silly like her. I hoped so.

We talked as we ate. We left questions about my mother and the house next door for Brenda and me to talk about later. The garlic bread was crunchy and warm, and it was hard not to slurp the spaghetti, although with that red tablecloth it wouldn't have been a problem. Along with Jake, we helped clear the table while Brenda loaded the dishwasher. Then Jake looked at his phone and checked the time.

"We need to get moving," he said, and Nicole, Jodi, and Emily got ready to leave.

"Don't be too late," Brenda said.

"OK, Mom," I thought to myself, and I smiled inside.

"Come into the family room," said Brenda as she flicked the switch on the gas fireplace. I thought of my grandmother who loved chopping and hauling wood. Would she welcome a gas fireplace or think it was the lazy person's way of keeping warm? I know I loved the smell of wood burning in a fireplace. Gas fireplaces lacked that smoky, woody smell, but I had to admit that a fire in this fireplace was a lot more convenient. We sank into a big couch in front of the fire, each of us holding a mug of hot tea.

"So, Mari, what do you want to know about your mom?"

"I never expected to meet you and find out you were such excellent friends with my mother. I've always had a million questions for her, but maybe you know some answers, like who lives in the houses nearby, but based on the moving curtains in the windows across the street, I think you have a nosey neighbor."

"That would be Mr. Rowland. He's lived here as long as I have. Keeps to himself, but very nosey."

"Did he know my mother, too? I guess he did if he was here then."

"He has been here for years. Of course, he knew who she was."

"Tears welled up inside me, and I tried to stop them because I knew then that the floodgates would open and I wouldn't be able to stop crying, and then I'd get nowhere with my questions, so I stared into the fire.

"First," I said, composing myself, "I need to know who's living in my old house now."

"Well, soon after you moved away, the house went on the market, but people knew the address because of the news stories, and it wasn't selling. Then your father must have dropped the price because the local police chief bought it. He's lived in it ever since."

"That sounds weird, the police chief buying a murder scene. Does he have a family?" I asked.

"No. He has a dog. A big German Shepherd."

"Why would he want to buy our house?" I asked. "I think if he saw the scene of my mother's murder, he wouldn't want to live there. He worked on solving the murder, didn't he?'

"Yes, he did. He was the chief investigator."

I thought maybe he bought the house so he could still work on the murder. But that would be strange. Maybe it was just because it was a bargain. That was less strange. I could identify with shopping for a bargain, but still, it was weird.

"I think I want to talk to him," I said. "Maybe he could tell me some things I don't know."

"Well, good luck with that," she said. "He's not the friendliest guy. I haven't heard him talk about the murder for years. Nobody talks about it anymore. Lots of people who remember it moved away. I'm the only one left on Windthorne who lived here when it happened. Oh, and Mr. Rowland across the street."

"What about your husband?"

"My husband?" Her expression changed completely. "He and I split up the year after your mother died. He left Danbury, and Jake and I haven't heard from him since. He left his job, packed his clothes, and left. I don't even know where he went."

"Wow," I said. "That's got to hurt."

"It did," she said. "But I had Jake to take care of, and I had to work to support us, and I didn't have time to concentrate on how I felt."

I guess I could understand. I was curious about her husband, but I wasn't comfortable asking her questions about her marriage. It really wasn't any of my business and probably had nothing to do with my mother's murder since her husband left the following year. I needed to know how much Brenda knew about what had happened to my mother. I pushed on with what I thought were the most important questions.

"So, what do you remember about my mother's murder? Maybe something happened in the days before?"

"It was fifteen years ago, Mari. Some memories are very vivid, some are cloudy. The most vivid was when the police came to our door that night. When my husband opened the door, they told us that there was a break-in next door, and they wanted to know if we had seen or heard anything during the day. Then they wanted to question us further and told us someone had murdered your mother. I couldn't believe it. She was my friend. How could that happen? I remember that they knew that she had been dead for a while. Your father found her, and he was an emotional mess. Who wouldn't be? Finding his wife in bed with an ax in her head had to be horrible. The police wanted to bring him in and question him. I asked about you and they told me you were okay, but you and your dad needed a place to stay, so we offered you our spare room. They planned on meeting with your dad the next day, so he needed somebody to take care of you. I offered to do it, but I wondered what had happened to your grandmother."

"My grandmother?" I asked. "She wasn't there."

"Yes, she was. She was visiting your parents that week. I thought she might want to babysit you, but it turned out that she had left the day before to go back to Rochester. You and your father stayed with us for a few days, and he made funeral arrangements so that once the coroner released the body, they could take your mother back to Rochester to bury her."

I guessed it was the coroner's job to figure out the cause of death. I assumed that it would be obvious given how she died. But then I remembered watching all those CSI shows where the medical examiners looked for clues. I made a mental note to contact the medical examiner about the report. I hoped I could get it.

"I've never seen her grave," I said. "I don't think anyone from my family goes there. Or maybe they go but just don't tell me." I decided that when I got home, I would go to the cemetery to see where they buried her.

"Well, your father was very emotional, so your grandparents came to help him and you on the trip to Rochester. I guess your grandmother had just gotten home when they got the news, so she got back in the car to make the trip back here. They were pretty upset. I was a wreck, too. She was my best friend."

"Did they stay here?" I asked.

"No. I had no more room, so they stayed in a hotel until they released the body."

She told me how the local newspapers covered the story.

"It was sensational," she said. "There had never been a murder as vicious as that in this area before. It was horrible. Some people were sure it was a robbery gone bad. Others thought it was someone your mother knew. People began locking their doors and moving axes out of their garages and into their basements. The worst part was that some said your father did it."

There it was again. Was my father always going to be a suspect?

"What do you think?" I asked.

"I went through thinking it was each of those. I never could come to a strong conclusion. Now I think it's one of those 'cold cases' you hear about."

"You suspected my father?" I said.

"For a while, just like everybody did. The newspapers hinted at it, but nothing ever came of it and the investigation just seemed to end. People felt he shouldn't have left town, but where was he going to go? He needed to bury her, he needed to care for you, and your parents only lived in Danbury for a brief time. It made sense for him to go home to Rochester. Besides, who could live in a house where such a grisly murder took place?"

"Evidently the police chief," I said.

Maybe I should contact the reporter who covered the story. Maybe there would be leads there. Brenda refilled our mugs with hot tea, and I sank back into the couch.

"Just tell me more about my mother," I said. "Did she like to read? What was her favorite music? Did she like to cook? What kind of mom was she?"

"Haven't your father and grandparents ever told you all of this stuff?"

"No," I said. "They don't talk about her with me, and I don't ask them anymore. Besides, I know that my friends know more about me than my family does, so I figure that being such excellent friends with her, you'd know a lot more than my grandparents. Like I said, my father just says nothing."

"OK," Brenda said. "She loved poetry. The more romantic, the better. She told me her favorite subject in college was literature. She loved sad poems, like when someone was mourning the loss of love. We had a mini book club, she and I. We'd read a book and talk about it while we pushed our strollers around the neighborhood. She liked mysteries like Agatha Christie because she liked to imagine the furniture and clothes of the time, and she loved to guess the murderer in the first twenty pages. She wrote her guess down on an index card and used the card as her bookmark so that when she figured it out, she left the card in the book at that page."

I made a mental note to read Agatha Christie. I should've brought my notebook to write these mental notes.

"She liked different types of music, but her favorite songs were those she could sing. She always had music on in the house. She sang to you all the time. She was a speech pathologist, and she believed it would help you develop language. She sang nursery rhymes and children's songs like they sang on Sesame Street. She insisted that the words in the songs had to be clear so you could understand them and learn them. She sang songs by Frank Sinatra or Ella Fitzgerald. They were from an earlier time, but she loved that music."

I could listen to Brenda tell me about my mother all night because her stories showed me what a great mom I had and how much she did for me. I made another mental note to find some Sinatra or Ella Fitzgerald to listen to. Maybe I'd even make a playlist so I could listen to her music whenever I wanted.

"Mari, your mother was an intelligent woman. She read, she kept up with politics not just here in this town, but she knew what was going on in the world. She voted in every election, even the little ones. If we argued about politics, it would never break up our friendship. We had a lot of fun together as couples, too. Sometimes we went over to your house for a glass of wine or two and some conversation. The four of us laughed and told stories while you and Jake slept. We all were wonderful friends."

"And what about my dad?" I asked.

"At that time? Gee, Mari. I remember him as being very serious. This job he had was important to him and he spent a lot of time at work–a lot of late evenings. Your mother said it was important to him to do an expert job, but she wanted to spend more time together as a family. I think it was a 'thing' between them. She was spending her time at home taking care of you and she wanted more from him. She complained to me when it got to her, and I could always tell when they had an argument over it the night before."

"You said she was a speech pathologist."

"She was. She worked with kids with disabilities in the schools. She loved the job and worked until the end of the school year before you were born, but she stayed home with you afterwards."

It was getting late, and we heard the door open. Jake walked in.

"Are you two still talking?" he said.

"I'd better get going," I told him. "How was the concert?"

"It was fantastic. My friend's band was the opening act, and they were awesome. Jodi, Nicole, and Emily sang along with everyone and seemed to have an excellent time. We went for coffee, spent some time getting to know each other better, and I dropped them at the hotel. Can I ask you–is Emily seeing anyone?"

I shook my head no and smiled. Once again, I made a mental note, this time to tell Emily that Jake had asked about her. Then I turned to Brenda to thank her, not just for dinner, but for our conversation. I told her I might stop by again before we left, and she gave me an enormous hug and a kiss on my forehead.

"Anytime. Please stay safe," she said.

I left and drove to the hotel. My friends were all gathered in the room Emily and I shared. They were lying on the beds, and it looked like they were getting ready to have a pajama party.

I went off to change into my pajamas so that I could join in the festivities, then said, "Time to report in."

"The concert was great," Nicole said. "Did you know that the school has a great music program? Jake told me that Danbury was the home of Charles Ives. Not that I had ever heard of him before, but they named the music center after him. After we left the campus, we went to this coffee shop nearby where we talked about you."

"What did you say about me? I can tell you're making that up."

Emily looked at the others, who were smiling. "It isn't always all about you, you know."

"Emily, not that I want to sound like a fourth grader, but I need to tell you that Jake likes you! He asked me if you were seeing anyone."

Emily had a huge smile on her face. "Really? Don't you all think he is *so cute*?"

"Adorable," said Nicole, rolling her eyes.

"The cutest," said Jodi, making kissing noises.

"The nicest," I said. And regardless of the others making fun, I really believed it.

"Are we going to see him tomorrow?" asked Emily.

"I don't know," I said. "You tell me."

"Maybe we could stop by his house," Emily proposed.

"I don't know, Em. Would that be like stalking?" I kidded her. "Maybe you should text him to give him a warning. You exchanged numbers, right?

She picked up her phone, typed quickly, and waited. The phone gave off a ding and her eyes went right to the screen.

"Ok! We're all set. He needs to work tomorrow night, but he says we should stop by in the morning around ten."

"We'd better get to sleep," I said. "We leave tomorrow and it's a long drive. Plus, I need to stop by the campus to pick up some information and do a quick tour."

Chapter 13

The next morning, we packed up, had our free breakfast, checked out of the hotel, and then headed straight for Brenda's house at 41 Windthorne Road. She greeted us with hot coffee and a warm hello, and Jake came downstairs and herded my friends into the family room. I stayed with Brenda in the kitchen.

"Tell me about the guy living in my old house. The chief of police. Could you introduce me to him?"

"Sure," she said. "I'll call him now." And she did. When he answered the phone, he told her to bring me over.

We left Jake and my friends and went next door. As we walked to the front door of 43 Windthorne, I saw the curtains move in the front window of the house across the street. The ever-present nosey neighbor. I had wanted time to plan my visit with the chief, so I was feeling unsettled because he was home, he'd invited me over, and I would soon see his house– my house– the house where my mother was murdered. I had no plan, no list of questions, and it frightened me to do this, but I had to go. He greeted us and shook my hand.

"Mari, it's good to see you. The last time I saw you, you were a baby. Come on in and sit down. Can I get you something?"

He was a tall man, bald, and I think he shaved his head like a lot of police officers. The visible stubble on his head was gray. Although he was probably in his late sixties, he looked like he was in very good shape. He had a serious face with more frown lines than laugh lines, and he wore gold-rimmed glasses that framed his brown eyes. I imagine that if he came to arrest me for something, I'd figure that by the look on his face I must have done something wrong even if I wasn't sure of what it was. The house, or at least what I could see of it from my limited range of vision, appeared spotless and neat. Not much furniture. There were no pictures on the walls. The furniture consisted of a leather couch with a built-in recliner, a coffee table, two additional armchairs and a television.

"My name is Ted Langdon in case Brenda hasn't told you. Most people call me 'Chief' even though I retired about five years ago. Are you okay with dogs? I have a German Shepherd named Buddy, but he's in his crate. Would it be okay with you if I let him out?"

"Sure. I really love dogs. I don't have one of my own, but my best friend does."

In about five seconds I was being sniffed by Buddy, who lay down next to me and put his head on my feet. Even though Chief Langdon did a lot to put me at ease, I wasn't comfortable, and I was glad Brenda was with me. The dog helped too.

"So how can I help you?" he said.

I almost started crying because I had finally arrived here, in my family home, the place where my mother was killed. It all seemed like too much, but I needed to take it all in.

"You know, I was one of the first people to arrive after your father called 911 and I helped investigate the murder, but I'm frustrated that I haven't been able to solve it."

"Can I ask you to show me where my mother was when you got here? Do you mind if I take pictures?"

"Sure, you can take pictures. I hope you'll be okay with this, Mari," he said with a gentle tone in his voice. "It's a tough situation for you to be in." He put his hand on my shoulder.

Brenda and I followed him upstairs to the bedrooms. All the doors on the second floor were closed, but he walked up to one door and unlocked it. Buddy stayed close by my side while Brenda took my hand.

I cannot describe the feeling as I walked into that room. It was like my breath was sucked out of me. The room was chilly. But the weirdest thing was my locket. It got very, very warm. I put my hand on it and felt its warmth, and just held onto it as I looked around the room. There was an enormous difference between the chilly temperature of the room and the warmth of my locket. The room had no furniture. The walls were deep red, and the floors were highly polished. I walked over to a set of French doors opening to a small balcony overlooking the backyard, which had a deep green lawn surrounded by a six-foot fence backed with tall pine trees. How pretty. How quiet. How private. No one could see into that yard. Had the murderer come into the house that way? How often had my mother looked out the windows into that yard? I stood there for a few minutes just taking it all in. I imagined the horror that happened there. My chest was tight, and I was still finding it hard to breathe. I asked Chief Langdon why the room was empty and why the walls were red.

"Mari, I live here alone. I don't use this room and if you noticed, it's always freezing. Maybe because of the doors. I don't know. I don't want to sleep in here, even though it's the biggest bedroom. I painted it red because even though we hired professional cleaners, they couldn't get the blood out of the walls. I'm sorry to tell you this, but I painted over the blood to hide it. I also had to replace the floor."

I swallowed hard, and then I asked him, "Why do you keep the door locked? There's nothing in here." I took out my phone and snapped some pictures of the room, with its red walls and shiny wood floors.

"Just some additional security. A murder took place here and people were curious. They came at all hours of the day and night. Before I moved in, the house had been broken into two or three times."

At that moment, I felt sick. I'm not sure if it was the chilly room or the details that got to me, but I needed to lean into Brenda. She put her arm around me and led me out of my mother's bedroom. I asked Chief Langdon if I could see the nursery.

This room was unlocked and was right next door to the master bedroom. It was much smaller and painted a soft pink. One wall had cute wallpaper with little kittens, puppies and flowers on it. Even though the wallpaper had faded, the room had an enormous window, which made it warm and bright. Perfect for a baby girl! I took some more pictures. Chief Langdon was almost smiling.

"Mari, this is the original wallpaper that your mother put up."

Brenda agreed. "I remember when she picked it out. And even though she was six months pregnant, she hung it herself. Your father was furious that she was climbing a ladder."

My eyes filled up, and my nose began running.

Unlike the other bedroom, this room wasn't empty. Sitting in the center of the room was a dusty white high-back wicker rocking chair with a faded pink checked cushion. Brenda said, "Your dad bought it for her at a garage sale. She painted it and made the cushion herself so she could sit there and rock you when she fed you. And as you got older, she sat here with you in her lap while she read stories to you."

I snapped a picture, and then I sat in the chair. I closed my eyes for a minute and imagined my mother holding me, reading to me, singing to me. Chief Langdon and Brenda looked at each other and then the Chief whispered, "Come on, Mari. Let's go downstairs."

Walking away, I went with them into the hallway. But then I stopped. "I want to go back for one more minute." They stood at the top of the stairs waiting for me. I opened the door and looked back in at the pink walls, the cute wallpaper, and the white chair. As I watched, I thought I saw the chair start to rock. I turned away while Chief stepped to the doorway and closed the door, and then we all went downstairs.

The reality of my mother's murder had never been this strong. Sure, I missed her, but I had been nowhere where I could feel her around me like this. I sat down on the Chief's couch to gather my thoughts. Brenda sat next to me, and Chief Langdon was across from me in an armchair. Buddy returned to sit at my feet. I was trembling from head to toe.

"Chief, you worked on this case from the very beginning. Fifteen years have gone by. You must have some idea about who did this!" I was upset, and I was furious. I stood up and started pacing. Buddy got up and followed me. My voice got louder with every word I spoke. "WHO?" I said at the top of my voice, "I have to know WHO KILLED MY MOTHER?"

There was no answer.

The Chief sat there looking straight ahead. "I wish I knew," he whispered. I could hear the frustration in his voice. I was still standing when Brenda put her arms around me and said, "Mari, come on. I think we need to go. Goodbye, Chief. Thanks for the tour."

We went back to Brenda's house where Nicole, Jodi, Emily, and Jake were waiting. I still hadn't calmed down, and I told them all what had happened.

Brenda made us lunch to give me time to compose myself. Lunch calmed me down, but at this moment, I was in no shape to drive. Everyone was quiet, maybe because they were eating, I don't know. Emily suggested that we leave and go to the college to pick up some information and then start the trip home. I was torn. I wanted to stay to find out more, and at the same time I wanted to go home. We all thanked Brenda, and she hugged each of us. She told me I was welcome to stay at her house if I wanted to come back to continue my search. We took a few group selfies, and I gave my phone to Nicole to take a picture of me in the driveway of my house. I looked at the house across the street and saw a man's face peeking out from behind the living room curtains. Mr. Rowland was on the lookout.

We went to the car, but Emily and Jake hung back. He took Emily's hand, and I thought I saw him give it a squeeze. She smiled at him and then got in the car.

After we had driven away, I said, "Good for you, Em. Jake is perfect for you. He was so nice to all of us, especially to you guys. Where does he want to go to college?"

"He thinks the University of Connecticut. I'll look at it, too."

"Woooooooo!" Everybody said at once. And we all started laughing. What a relief to be with my friends who could make me laugh again!

We drove around both campuses of the college, took some photos and began our drive home. Emily offered to drive for the first leg of the trip, and I was fine with that, because I wanted to process what had happened this morning. I took out my journal and wrote a letter to my mother.

> *Dear Mom,*
>
> *This trip has been very hard but very good for me. It was good to meet your friend Brenda and her son Jake. (Em was even happier than I was to meet him!) Our house was probably very different from the way you had it when we lived there. You were such a warm person, I think. But Chief Langdon, who lives there now, was kind of cold, and the house was cold, too. Even my nursery with its pink walls and sweet animal wallpaper was cold. I know your spirit was sitting in the rocking chair this morning. I even thought I saw the chair rocking. I hated that your bedroom was red to hide your blood, so terrible. I wonder what the room looked like before that day. I wonder what the other two bedrooms look like. I'll need to come back. I need to find your murderer and you need to show me where to look.*
>
> *I love you,*
> *Mari.*

I closed the book and closed my eyes. I pictured my mother sitting in her rocking chair holding me, and I fell asleep as Em drove us back toward Albany.

Chapter 14

The four of us arrived in Albany in the late afternoon. I felt good after I woke up from my nap, so Em and I switched places. Jodi and Nicole curled up in the back seat while I drove and thought about the things I needed to do when I got home, like read Agatha Christie mysteries, check music apps for songs by Frank Sinatra and Ella Fitzgerald, maybe make a playlist for myself, and figure out a way to get back to Connecticut to do some more detective work.

I was in a weird mood. I was happy that I had met Brenda. I felt so comfortable with her, and I understood why my mother was friends with her. Seeing our old house was scary. And Chief Langdon was unsettling, too. It was a mixed bag of feelings. I wanted to put my feelings away and get back to the scary experiences of my friends as a distraction. Somehow, if everyone was in a scary state of mind, we had a bond to share. I asked Em to tell us about her scariest experience.

At first, she was silent. Then she said, "I need you to keep this just between the four of us. Got it?"

"We promise," we all said. And then Emily's story began.

"I think you guys know that I have an Uncle Pete."

"Yeah, we do," Nicole said. "I think we all met him at your house last year."

Emily spoke slowly and in a low voice. "Uncle Pete really isn't my uncle. He's a friend of my parents."

"And…" we said. Our voices got low also.

Emily went on, "Uncle Pete always made me feel uncomfortable when he was around."

"How?" asked Jodi. "What did he do?"

"He was kind of creepy, like trying to flirt with me, and when he came to visit my parents, he'd kiss my mother on the cheek, but he aimed for my mouth when it was my turn. I had to turn my head fast to get away."

"EEEEW!" we yelled, practically in unison.

"He's about the same age as your father," I said.

"Gross," said Nicole and Jodi, "What did he do?"

Emily continued, "One night I was babysitting for my cousin when Uncle Pete called me. I don't know how he got my cell number, but he knew where I was, and he wanted to come over. I told him he couldn't, and he needed to leave me alone." He said, "Now Emily, it must be lonely babysitting. I just want to come over and keep you company. I'm just down the street."

"I got super scared. I said, 'No, and you'd better leave me alone because I'll tell my father.'" Uncle Pete laughed, said, "I'll see you soon," and hung up. I went to the doors and windows and made sure I locked them, and I closed the curtains. Then I called my dad and told him about Uncle Pete. 'Dad,' I said, 'I'm scared. I'm afraid he'll come here.' My father said, 'Don't worry, Em. I'll handle it. Just make sure you locked the doors and don't let him in.' Forty-five minutes later, my mother called. 'Emily, you can relax. Dad took care of Uncle Pete. He won't bother you anymore.'"

Nicole asked, "What did your father do to him?"

"I don't know," Em said, "but he never bothered me again, and he's not invited to any family parties anymore."

"And he never called you again?" I said.

"Nope. But I still get scared when I think about what could've happened."

"Wow, Em, I'm scared just listening to you talk about this guy," said Nicole. "You're lucky your dad was around to take care of this creep."

"My dad is the best," said Emily.

"You were strong yourself, Em. Dealing with him on the phone, calling your dad, locking the doors and windows, and even pulling the curtains. You were right on top of the situation," I said. "How do you feel about it now?" I reached over to pat her on the leg.

"It still feels creepy, but at least I don't need to be around him anymore."

I was trying to absorb the story she had told us, but I was very glad we were almost home. I had enough of scary stuff for today. We could talk more about Uncle Pete some other time whenever Em needed someone to listen.

By that time, we were passing through Syracuse, and I told everyone I needed their help to figure out how to get myself back to Danbury for another visit. There was no train that went directly there from Rochester, so I'd need to go by car. The chances of getting my grandmother's car again were slim.

"Em," I asked. "Are you planning to go to UConn to look around? It looks like Jake will be visiting there too."

"I hope so. I just need to talk to my parents about it. I guess you'll be looking for a ride to Connecticut, right? Mari seriously, talk to my dad about what you're trying to do. Maybe he can give you some advice."

"About going to Connecticut?" I said with a laugh.

"You know what I mean. Solving your mother's murder."

"I can ask my own father," I said.

"Mari, that doesn't make sense. Go to my dad. He's a police officer. What if your father killed her? He'll want to protect himself, and I'm worried that something might happen to you."

I got angry. "Em, stop talking about my dad that way." But then I thought about the story Emily just told us about Uncle Pete, how she handled him, and I took her advice to talk to her dad. Maybe he could give me some pointers.

We were finally back in Rochester, and I dropped off everyone at their houses. We all agreed it was a wonderful trip, despite it being so intense, and I was grateful that my friends went with me and supported what I wanted to do. I hugged each one of them goodbye. "Thanks, girls. You are the best," I said.

Everyone was waiting for me when I walked into the house. Grandma came over and gave me a hug.

"I'm glad you're home," she said. "You must be exhausted. How did it go? See any colleges you or your friends were interested in?"

I agreed with Grandma. I was exhausted, not just from the driving, but also from the intense emotions, meeting lots of new people connected to my family, and the emotional sharing with my friends in the car. I told everyone we could talk tomorrow, but I needed a good night's sleep. I was too tired to eat dinner, so I went upstairs, took a long, hot shower, and put on some warm, flannel pajamas. I climbed into bed, but before falling asleep, I checked my email. There was a message from Brenda.

> *Hi Mari,*
>
> *Hope you got home ok. It was great to see you and your friends. I still can't believe how much you look like your mother. You brought back lots of memories!*
>
> *See you soon,*
>
> *Brenda.*

I was too tired to answer, so I'd send something tomorrow. I was feeling numb, and I fell into a deep sleep. I didn't dream; I didn't move, and I never woke until the alarm went off the next morning. It was hard to open my eyes. I rolled onto my back and stayed in bed for a couple of minutes. Realizing that it was a school day, I finally pushed back the blankets and got up. I could smell breakfast cooking as I got dressed, and when I finished, I walked toward the smell of bacon and eggs.

"How was your trip?" Dad asked as Grandma put a plate in front of me. The bacon and eggs smelled great, and I was starving. I told the three of them about the driving, the hotels and the colleges and I got out my phone and showed them the pictures of the colleges we visited.

Grandpa asked, "Did you get to Danbury?"

"We did, and I went to Windthorne Road to see the house." The three of them looked at each other and then back at me. It was a strange look, almost kind of sneaky, as if they had a secret that they shared. They looked at each other, but they wouldn't make eye contact with me. I pulled up the photos I took of the front of the house. I wasn't ready to share the inside pictures with them yet, but I showed them the pictures of Brenda and Jake.

"Brenda still lives there?" Grandma seemed surprised by that. "I thought she might have moved."

"You know her husband left, don't you?" I asked.

"I guess I didn't." She looked surprised.

No comment from Dad or Grandpa. By then it was time to leave for school.

"Can we talk later?" Dad asked.

"Sure. I'll be home at the regular time. See you at supper."

I left them all sitting at the breakfast table looking stunned. I wondered what they would say to each other after I left the room. Would they finish eating or would the bacon and eggs wind up in the garbage disposal because they were too distracted by what I had told them and the pictures on my phone? I walked out into the chilly October morning, which felt much colder than the actual temperature, not because of any wind chill but because my emotions were right on the surface of my skin.

Emily was waiting and we walked to school without saying much. You could smell Fall in the air. We joined up with Nicole and Jodi, who also were quiet. The one thing we all asked Em was if she heard from Jake. Turns out they were texting last night and working on planning a time to see each other when Em and her family went to Connecticut to visit UConn. They hadn't set a time yet, but Em planned to talk to her parents tonight. Maybe Thanksgiving?

"Thanksgiving seems good," I said. "Maybe you could plan to go the week before, so you'd have more time."

"I guess you want to go with us," Emily said.

"If your parents are okay with it, and if I want to go to Danbury and your parents let me come with you, you'd need to drop me off at Brenda's house. Then you could see Jake, too." I looked at Em out of the corner of my eye with a little mischief on my mind. She smiled back at me.

"How does that sound?" I said.

No comment from Emily, just a smile, sort of like the one on the Mona Lisa. Real subtle.

My friends and I spent our day yawning our way through our classes. I was feeling ambivalent about going home that night, about answering questions about our trip, and asking my family questions now based on stuff I had learned while I was in Danbury. But there was no way around it, not if I wanted to solve my mother's murder. I also had to get to work on my to-do list, finding out if I could get the coroner's report, doing some on-line searches for newspaper reports about the murder, finding the reporter who wrote the story, finding out all I could about the Chief and Brenda and her husband. And what about the nosey neighbor across the street? Then I remembered Brenda's email. I checked my messages and there was another message from Brenda.

Hi, Mari,

I hope I have the right email address for you because I didn't hear from you last night. Text me so I know you got this and I have the right address.

Brenda.

I felt a little guilty that I didn't answer her, so I typed,

Hi Brenda,

Yes, we got home safely, and everything is okay. Will get back to you soon. *Mari."*

Dinner that night started out quietly. Grandma started the conversation.

"So, tell us about the trip, Mari."

And I did.

But I left out lots of facts; I didn't tell them about meeting Chief. I didn't tell them about being in the house or seeing the bedrooms. I didn't tell them about the rocking chair. But I told them about meeting Brenda and Jake, about talking with Brenda about my mother, about planning to go back at Thanksgiving. I gave them just a little information.

"It was a great trip," I told them. "The house seemed a lot smaller than I thought it was."

"And what did you find out? You were pretty determined to find out what happened when your mother was killed," said Dad.

I could hear the tightness in his voice, as if he needed to clear his throat.

"Not much," I lied.

I had to give him credit for trying. I decided that I wouldn't tell them the details of what I found. It was a gut feeling that I had. My gut was churning, and I took that as a message from it telling me I should just keep quiet until I had more information. Usually when my gut talks to me it doesn't expect a reply, and even if it did, I wouldn't think it was necessary to justify what I left out or put in. Especially with my mother's murder.

It was interesting to watch everyone as we sat at the table. Each time I told them something about the trip, Grandma looked at Dad and Dad looked at Grandpa who looked over at Grandma. It was like the end of a scene in a soap opera when the camera closes in on the face of one person reacting to an important line in the script. I could almost hear that soap opera music playing in the background–da-dummmm!

We finished dinner and after we cleaned up, I went to my room to do some homework and spend some time on the computer. Just as I sat down to work, I got a text from Emily.

Guess who's coming to town.

I almost wrote, "Santa Claus."

Who?

Jake and his mother. He's coming to look at the colleges here next Friday.

OMG, Em. That was fast. I knew we'd try to see them again, but just within a week? That'll be great. I can spend more time with Brenda, and you can hang out with Jake!

Sounds perfect to me, Em responded with a heart emoji.

I told my family that Brenda and Jake were coming to Rochester. I thought their reactions were interesting. They looked at me and each other, then Grandma said, "It will be nice to see them. I haven't seen them since…well, since your mother died. Do they have a place to stay?"

I really hoped she would not offer them to stay at our house. I wanted to spend time alone with Brenda, which would be difficult with my family around. Probably Jake and Emily wanted some alone time, too.

"I am sure they'll stay in a hotel, Grandma."

"Well," she said, "Maybe they'd like to come for dinner one night. I'd hate not to see them. Maybe Em and her parents could come, too."

As she said that, she looked at Dad and Grandpa, who were silent. Grandma has always been the diplomat in the family. Always ready to offer a smile or a meal. Dad and Grandpa were so much alike. Quiet and stoic would be the best way to describe them. But something made little sense to me. Seeing Dad like this didn't match up with what Brenda had told me, how when she and her husband were with my parents, they had such a good time. How could that be? How did he go from being a fun person to one who had lost that sense of fun? I guess if somebody murdered your wife, it would do that.

Friday arrived, and Emily got a text from Jake with the name of the hotel where they were staying. I texted Brenda and invited them to our house for dinner.

That was the weirdest evening I'd ever had. First, I thought it was weird that Grandma was inviting Em's parents. Although they were friends with our family, what connected Brenda and Jake to my family was my mother's death. Em's parents, the Reeses, weren't connected in that way. Well, they knew about the murder, but never really asked about it. Did I mention that Mr. Reese was a police officer? That always seemed strange to me, that he never asked about my mother's murder, but maybe he didn't want to get involved in something he couldn't do much about or something that happened in another state. Anyway, Dad offered the adults some wine, and we sat around the fireplace before dinner.

Brenda told Grandma, "I love the smell of an actual fire. My fireplace is gas. Very convenient, but it doesn't have that authentic smell. And I really don't have the motivation to chop wood."

Grandma said, "I love chopping wood." She got up and threw another log onto the fire. "It's great exercise. But you look good, Brenda. You haven't changed a bit."

"You look great, also," Brenda said. "But I was so stunned to see Mari. She looks exactly like Marianne. I almost couldn't believe it. And there she was, standing in their old driveway at 43 Windthorne, just like her mother used to..."

And then the conversation stopped. Brenda stood up and said to me, "Mari, could I see your bedroom?"

I was surprised at her request, but then she said, "I need to go out to my car first. I have something for you." And she headed for the door. She returned with a cardboard box. "This is yours," she said. "But let's go upstairs to open it."

She followed me upstairs to my room carrying the box and put it on the bed. My attention went right to it. "What's in it?" I asked.

"These are books that belonged to your mother. I'm embarrassed to tell you she loaned them to me, but I never returned them. I found the box in my attic where I put it after you and your father left town. Mostly they're Agatha Christie mysteries, but there are some poetry books in there. Elizabeth Barrett Browning and Dorothy Parker. Your mother loved both. You should have them."

An old paper label on the top flap had Brenda's name and address on it. The cardboard had softened over the years, and the weight of the books caused it to wobble in my hands. When my family moved here after my mother died, I think they left everything behind except our clothes. I thanked Brenda, gave her a hug, and put the box under my bed so I could go through it later. Just then, Grandma appeared at the bedroom door. "Dinner's ready."

There was a definite chill in the air around the dinner table except for Jake and Em who, I am sure, were holding warm hands underneath it. I looked at everyone one at a time, trying to figure out what each person's relationship was to my mother. In this room were her husband, mother-in-law, father-in-law, best friend, and me. Em's mom was sitting stiffly in her chair, clearly wishing she was somewhere else. And Em's father seemed to look around at everyone, interested in watching the people around the table and listening to what little conversation there was.

And then it was over. Like a bunch of kids who just heard the dismissal bell ring, we all got up and cleared off the table, and Em and Jake went to Em's house to get the dog and take him for a walk. Em's parents said goodnight and left. Dad, my grandparents, Brenda, and I moved to the living room in front of the fireplace. Everyone had a cup of coffee, and Dad put a few fresh logs on the fire.

"So, Brenda," Dad said, "Where did Greg go after you split up?"

"Greg?" she said. "Jake's father? I really don't know."

"Really?" Dad said. "He just left, and you never heard from him again?" Frown lines appeared on his forehead.

"No, I never did," she said and looked into her coffee mug.

"That's weird."

"You're telling me!" she said as her eyes widened and flashed with anger. "It devastated me. I was all alone with a baby, no actual income, no real job. I haven't heard from him since he left. I don't know where he is, and I really don't care."

"Why did he leave?" Dad asked.

"I don't know, and I really don't want to talk about it. I need to go back to the hotel. Jake and I have a busy day tomorrow."

She stood up, picked up her phone and called him. "Jake, we need to go. Can you be ready to leave in five minutes?"

In a flash, her anger disappeared, and she looked at me with a weak smile. "Mari, I'd like to see you again. Would you like to be our tour guide tomorrow and show us how to get to the University?"

"Well," I said, "it's easy to find, but if you want me to go, I can do that. What time?"

"Nine o'clock?" There was a touch of annoyance in her voice. And then she left. I heard the car start and pull out of the driveway.

Dad went into the kitchen to help Grandma. I heard voices but couldn't quite make out what they were saying. As I walked toward the kitchen, I heard Dad say almost in a whisper, "I really don't want her around Mari, that's all."

I went upstairs and when I got to my room, my phone pinged. I checked the screen. It was a text from Brenda. *I'm sorry I left in a hurry and didn't get to spend more time with you. So glad we'll see each other tomorrow.*

I sent back a smiley face emoji and turned off the phone. I had lots to think about. I laid on my bed and reached into the box of books that Brenda brought me and took out an Agatha Christie novel, opened it, and before I finished the first page, I fell asleep.

Chapter 15

At 8:45 AM the doorbell rang. I was barely alert and glad Grandma was downstairs to let Brenda and Jake in. But they didn't come in. I heard voices downstairs and then I looked out the front bedroom window and saw them get back into the car. Jake moved to the back seat and closed the door. Grandma called up the stairs to me.

"They're here, Mari. Do you want to eat before you leave?"

"Just a bagel and juice," I said. "I don't think I'll be gone too long."

I ran down the stairs, putting on my denim jacket as I moved, took the bagel that Grandma had put in a plastic bag and drank the juice. I kissed her on the cheek and ran out the door to the car and slid into the front passenger seat.

"Hi, guys," I said. "Ready for the big tour?"

Brenda was almost bubbly this morning. "Where shall we go first?"

Jake was quiet. I got the sense that he wasn't into this. Maybe he wanted Emily to go instead of me. I was sure he'd rather be with her. She could've done this tour. I opened my big mouth and asked, "How come you asked me to go with you? Em could have done it and spent some time with you."

Jake still said nothing but just let out a quiet "hmmm" under his breath. He wasn't looking at me, but out the side window. Uh-oh. The difference in their moods showed some serious mother-son tension.

Brenda reached over and put her hand on my knee.

"Mari, I'm so happy to have connected with you. This was my decision. I wanted to spend as much time as I could with you. It brings back the time when your mother and I were close. Jake and Em can get together later today. We'll be here all weekend."

Jake said nothing, so I asked, "Jake, is this okay with you? Sounds quiet back there."

"It's okay," he sighed, but his voice was quiet, and I wasn't sure I believed him.

We got to the University and dropped Jake off at the Admissions Office. A tour group had formed outside, and Jake was absorbed into it as they took the sidewalk leading toward the library. I turned toward Brenda and she talked about my mother again.

"Your mother and I were pregnant at the same time. We went shopping together for wallpaper for the babies' rooms, and then we helped each other hang the paper. We bought fabric for curtains and your father bought her that rocking chair. It was a happy time for both of us. And when you and Jake were born, it was great. You were such a beautiful baby with your curly black hair. I always wanted a baby girl, and even though I was glad to have Jake, I must admit that I was a little jealous of your mother."

What a strange thing to say. Hm. I asked the big question. "Who do you think killed her?"

"I've thought about it ever since it happened, Mari. Maybe someone got into the house and did it. Maybe it was your father, maybe it was your grandmother, or my ex-husband. Or that nosey guy from across the street. Maybe it was the weird police chief. It could have been anybody."

"What about your ex-husband makes you think about him as the murderer?"

"I don't know." She sounded annoyed. She spoke faster and

faster. "I'm just making a list for you. You're so obsessed with this. I wish I could help you, but this is the best I can do. Mari, you need to put pressure on the police department. You should talk to Emily's dad. Jake says he's a policeman. Maybe he could give you some pointers about trying to work with them. But let's just enjoy being together. Is there someplace we could get some ice cream or coffee?"

I didn't want either, so I suggested that we just take a walk around the campus. Being with Brenda was making me feel uncomfortable. On the one hand, I wanted to know everything she knew, everything she felt when she was with my mother. On the other hand, I was feeling closed in. Was she using me as a replacement for my mother? I thought a walk in the fresh air would be the best for me. I needed to breathe. We walked around in silence. Something had changed between us and I wasn't sure what it was or why it changed. She was getting pushy. Lots of texts, and this visit so soon after we were in Danbury didn't seem like normal behavior to me. As we turned the corner, Jake came walking toward us.

"Are you ready to go?" he said.

"Are you?" his mother asked, looking at me.

"I am." I said, maybe a little too quickly.

As we got into the car, Jake took the driver's seat and said to Brenda, "I'll drop you off at the hotel and then I'll drive Mari home. I want to spend some time with Emily before we go back."

"Maybe we could spend some time together tomorrow, Mari," she said.

"I think I could do that," I said. I was torn between wanting to know more about my mother and not wanting to spend time with Brenda, but to do one thing, I'd need to do the other.

Jake and I dropped her off and went to Emily's house. She was glad to see us. Probably happier to see Jake than to see me, but she invited us both in and we sat in the living room.

"So, what did you think about the University?" I said.

"I have no intention of going there. Never did. I came here because my mother insisted. She wanted to visit you to see your family again. She was trying to talk me into the trip from the minute you all left Danbury. She's got this weird attachment to you."

"Just because of my mother's death?" I asked.

"No. It's something more and I can't figure it out. I know they were friends, but this seems like a lot, kind of like she wants you to be a replacement. She keeps telling me how much you look like your mother."

I wondered about that, too.

"Jake," I asked, "what about your father? Do you ever hear from him?"

"No. Never. It seems like he vanished off the face of the earth. I looked for him online, but there's no sign of him unless he changed his name or is just totally not into technology."

"And what about that weird police chief who lives next door to you in my old house? What's his story?" I asked.

"As far as I know, he's really into that murder."

"Why?" I said. "Is he determined to solve it?"

"I'm not sure. I guess so. He really is a friendly guy, at least to me. He hired me to mow his lawn and clean up outside. Occasionally, I'll help him with fix-up jobs around the house. My mother doesn't like him, but he cares a lot about this case. Otherwise, why would he invite you to his house and give you a tour?"

Emily asked, "So you've been upstairs? Mari said it was strange."

Jake replied, "He's got four bedrooms up there. They all have locks except your old nursery." He nodded my way.

"He showed me my parents' bedroom and the nursery when I was there. I figure one other bedroom is his, but what's in the fourth bedroom?" I asked.

Jake replied, "I've seen his bedroom because I helped him move some furniture up there. It's just a regular bedroom with regular bedroom furniture. Nothing crazy. But that last bedroom is a mystery to me. I don't know, maybe it's just storage."

"How could we find out?" I asked. "Maybe you could sneak in there and look." Once I finished saying that Emily snapped her head around to face me. Her eyes were wide open with a flash of anger.

"You can't ask Jake to spy on him for you," she said. "What if he got caught?"

"Yeah," Jake said. "It would be impossible to spy on him and get away with it. Don't forget, he's a police chief who is really into security. I've seen a couple of cameras around the outside of the house, so I'm sure he's got some planted inside, too. He already told you how he keeps what he calls 'the murder scene' locked because people were breaking in to see it."

"I think we all need to think about this a lot before we do anything stupid or before we ask Jake to do something stupid," said Emily.

We all agreed that this was important, and we got Jake to agree that he wouldn't do anything until we figured out how to do it without getting caught. And then I had an idea. "Why don't I just ask the chief to tell me what's in the other room?" I blurted this out to Jake and Emily, and we all started laughing.

"That's bold," said Emily, "such a radical approach. How are you going to do that?"

"Well, I could call him or maybe send him a letter or an email. Jake, do you have his address?"

"Sure," he said grinning, "43 Windthorne."

With my eyes squinted and my mouth screwed up, I looked at him and said, "I think I knew that one, Jake. I meant his email."

"No, I don't know it so you may have to try the pony express version. I can give you his phone number and you can text him."

Emily joined in. "You should write to him, Mari. A letter that asks him all the questions you want answered. You can make it clear, and if you take a few days to write it, maybe you can add to it when more questions come up."

That's what I did.

Chapter 16

I left the two lovebirds and walked home. Grandma and Grandpa were watching TV. Dad was in the little room off the kitchen he uses as an office, and he was on his laptop.

"Hi Dad. What are you up to?"

"Just checking my email and paying a few bills."

He was sitting at the small desk, and I sat down in the chair opposite him.

"Can we talk about something?"

"Sure," he answered as he closed his laptop.

"Did you know the police chief in Danbury before Mom's murder?"

"Not really. He was only an investigator back then. I saw him at meetings or around town, but we weren't friends, if that's what you're asking."

"Did he work on the investigation of Mom's murder?"

"Yes, he did. He was pretty committed to finding out who murdered her, and he and the other police investigators were all over me and the house. Then they even came here to interview us."

"You mean he came here?"

"Not him, just the investigators who worked with him. Then, when they found nothing, he backed off. But it seemed weird that when the crime scene tape came down and the house went on the market, he bought it. It went for a good price because of the murder. I just wanted to get rid of it because it had such awful memories, but I was still very surprised when he bought it. He paid cash, too. I knew what he earned. They had debated those salaries at the city budget meetings. It didn't seem like he made enough to have that kind of money on hand."

"Why do you think he bought it?"

"I thought about it a lot. Was it that important to him to solve the case that he would buy the house so he could keep studying it to find the killer? Who knows? I'm not a cop, but I thought they should look outside of the house for more clues. I'm sure he had other cases that he was working on too, but I had no evidence that he went to that extreme to solve other crimes. As far as I know, he wasn't in the habit of buying crime scenes."

"I met the chief, Dad. I was even inside his house. He gave me a tour."

Dad looked directly at me. His eyes got enormous, and his lips tightened. I could hear him breathing, or rather holding his breath. Was he going to yell at me? He looked both surprised and angry at the same time. He leaned on the table with both hands as if he planned to stand up, but he didn't. He leaned back in the chair and dropped his pen on the desk and folded his arms across his chest.

"Why did you go there? Are you crazy?" He gazed at me with flashing eyes.

"Why would you think that was crazy? I've told you how much I really need to know all this stuff and the only way to find out is to see for myself."

His voice got louder. "Nobody knows who killed your mother. You need to be careful about this quest you're on. What if you wound up with the murderer? What if he tried to kill you, too?"

"Do you mean that you think the chief killed Mom?"

"I never said that." Dad stood up and paced around the room. Every five steps he stopped and turned and looked at me. He walked back and forth, moving his hands in front of him like he was giving a lecture. It even sounded like a lecture as he went on.

"You need to stay away from him, that's all." He looked directly at me.

"Why?" I persisted, even though I knew Dad didn't want to keep the conversation going.

"Because he's creepy, that's all. End of story."

"Don't you want to know what I saw in there?"

"I lived in that house for three years. I know what it looks like and I don't want to think about it. When I do, all I see is your mother's body."

I stood up, too, ready to face him and stand my ground. "Brenda was with me, Dad. She stayed with me the whole time. I'm not stupid."

"I'm not so sure about Brenda, either." Dad said. "Don't do stupid things. You're taking a colossal risk here."

"I need to go back there again. I still have lots of questions."

He sat down, looked away from me and opened his laptop. The conversation was over.

I got a cup of tea and went to sit in front of the fire with my journal. As I watched the flames and warmed my hands on my cup, I let my mind wander. Why would anyone ever want to murder someone? I put my hand around the locket on my neck as I wrote a list of what I could see as reasons.

Reasons for Murder:

Revenge

Anger

Jealousy

Hatred

Accident

To save another person

In war

If you were crazy

To stop someone from doing something

Self-defense.

This was as far as I got. I decided to keep this list. If I thought of anything else, I could add it later. This might help me narrow down the list of suspects.

I thought about murder, taking someone's life away. How do you do that? What happens to your mind and heart that makes you want to murder somebody? And how do you do it so violently? But then again, the act of taking away someone's life was violent, even if it wasn't bloody. I guess you needed to intend to do that, to take a life, except if it was an accident. Maybe it was just an impulse. Should I add this one to my list? Maybe someone didn't intend to do it when they got up that morning, but now here they were, having murdered someone. Maybe it was planned, maybe they planned for a long time until they got the details right, not only to make sure they killed the person but also to make sure they didn't get caught. My brain was working overtime on this, and I got on my laptop to write a letter to the chief. I began it like a thank-you note.

Dear Chief Langdon,

Thank you for spending time with me when I was in Danbury and thank you for letting me spend time in your house. I am wondering if you would talk to me some more about what happened to my mother. It is very important to me. Can you email me or call me? Maybe we could Skype or Facetime.

Mari Franklin

I enclosed my phone and email address, put the note in an envelope with my return street address, stamped it and put it in the mailbox. He'd have it in a couple of days. All I needed to do was wait for him to get back to me.

Chapter 17

It was homecoming weekend at school, so there was plenty to do. In the morning there was a parade through town. We'd all worked on the huge class float with a fake moving van made of tissue paper flowers. A good theme to show how the senior class was all moving out at the end of the year. We wore overalls and carried cardboard boxes and stacks of books to symbolize going off to college. After the parade, there was a lunch party in the gym with food and music, and they gave awards for the best floats. We got first prize because as seniors, it was the last chance for us to win. In the afternoon we had our traditional football game. To be honest, we weren't the best team, but at least we scored. We lost, but the score was 21-13 which was not too shabby for us.

That night we had a dinner dance. Emily invited Jake, and Jodi, Nicole and I went together. We had no dates, but that was fine with us (or at least with me). I just wanted to experience the crowd. As we got closer to graduation, it became more and more important to me to notice these events and take pictures in my heart of my friends and this high school. Besides, my focus wasn't to find a date, but it was to find the person who killed my mother. The gym was lit up with fairy lights and the DJ was outstanding. He had us singing along to a lot of songs, and we danced in groups. We held up our phones with the flashlights on and the crowd swayed back and forth to the slow music. I knew I wouldn't forget Homecoming.

The next day, Sunday, was a pancake brunch hosted by the Rotary Club. Dad and Grandpa were members and helped serve the crowds that showed up. They volunteered every year. There were long tables covered with plastic tablecloths in the school colors. There were heated serving pans full of sausages and bacon. Members of the Rotary Club were stationed at grills and were making pancakes by the hundreds. There were pitchers of orange juice and beakers of syrup. Pats of butter wrapped in gold foil were in little bowls on each table. Always the same menu and usually the same people. After the brunch, all the alumni who had come for the weekend left for home and so did we, although we lived a lot closer. Emily, Jake, and I went to Em's house to hang out.

"Just to let you know, I wrote to the chief and asked him if we could talk about my mom. I'm sure it'll take a few days for him to get back to me," I told them. "I'll let you know when I hear."

"Be careful, Mari," Em said.

"I agree," said Jake. "If you need any help, let Em or me know."

"I'll be careful," I said. "I let my dad know what was going on, but he's really upset with me for going to the chief's house even though Jake and Brenda were there."

I got up slowly, not wanting to leave my friends, but understanding that they wanted some time alone together before Jake had to leave.

"Oh, and Jake," I said, "Please don't tell your mother that I contacted the chief. I'd rather keep that to myself for now."

"Sure, Mari."

Brenda arrived to pick up Jake for their return home. Grandma offered to fill Brenda's travel mug, and Jake went over to Emily's for one last goodbye. I stepped to the car to say goodbye to Brenda.

"Have a safe trip. Thanks for bringing me Mom's books," I said.

"No problem, Mari. Please stay in touch. I wish you luck in solving your mother's murder."

The tone in her voice seemed funny to me, kind of sarcastic, as if she was sure I would never succeed.

At that moment, Jake and Em came out of Em's house holding hands. He kissed her goodbye and walked around to the passenger side of the car and got in.

"I'll text you on the way home," he said to Emily. He turned toward me and looked at me with a very serious face. "Be careful, Mari, he said. "I'll see you soon."

"I'm planning on it."

Brenda put the car into drive and off they went.

Homecoming weekend was the first big celebration of senior year. When we went back to school on Monday, I could feel a change in my senior classes. There seemed to be a hum in the air. Maybe our engines were running toward June and graduation. Maybe it was a sense that being high school graduates and adults was just around the corner. Or maybe there was that underlying fear about leaving home and proving yourself in the world that excited us with all the activity and quieted us at the same time as we thought about our futures. It was a distinct change in atmosphere, that's all. To me, remembering was the most important part.

After school I went home and went upstairs to write in my journal. I wanted to write to my mom about the weekend. I didn't realize how many things we packed into those two very full days. Between Homecoming and Brenda and Jake's visit, there was not a free minute. Now I just wanted to think and unwind from all the activities.

But as I wrote, my eye caught the last entry where I listed the reasons that someone would murder someone else. I read them again.

Revenge
Anger
Jealousy
Hatred
Accident
To save another person

In war
If you were crazy
To stop someone from doing something
Self-defense.

I wrote my journal entry to my mother. As I wrote, my other hand reached to touch the locket around my neck to feel my mother's presence with me.

Dear Mom,

I am looking at the list of reasons someone would commit murder, and I thought I'd ask YOU about who you think was the murderer.

Who wanted revenge? What happened that caused somebody to want to get even with you?

Who was angry with you? Why were they angry? It had to be a tremendous anger for someone to kill you over it.

Who was jealous? That could be lots of people. It sounds like you had an enjoyable life and lots of people would be jealous.

And hate. Wow, another powerful emotion. Who could hate you?

I could leave out an accidental reason. People don't get murdered the same way you did by accident. It had to be deliberate. Maybe I'll just put that aside for a while.

And who would kill you to save someone else? Who would they be trying to save from you?

War? No. That doesn't apply here at all unless you were battling with someone over a cause or an ideal.

If the murderer was crazy. I'm not sure, but I think to kill somebody, especially in the way they killed you, the killer would have to be crazy. Crazy because you were you, a nice and good person from what people say. I am not crazy, and I could never imagine doing such a thing.

To stop you from doing something. But what were you doing that upset them so much that they needed to stop you from doing it? Were you involved in something bad? No, I can't imagine that. Maybe you were doing something good, something idealistic, maybe a cause you worked for.

If it was self-defense, what would you have been doing to threaten them? I don't think anyone ever found a weapon that you would have used. Besides, what would you be doing at that hour of the morning threatening someone?

Well, that's the list. Just writing to you about it helps me to clear my brain. I am waiting to hear from the police chief. Maybe I'm getting closer.

Love,

Mari.

Chapter 18

Waiting for the chief to get back to me was almost painful. I checked the mail. I checked the voicemail on the house phone. I checked the email on my phone about a thousand times a day. Maybe he would ignore my message. Maybe he didn't want to talk to me anymore. At least he could have let me know! I had just about given up when I finally got an email from him.

Hello Mari,

I'll be happy to meet with you to talk. I am planning on attending a police conference in early December in Rochester. If you are available, I could meet with you then. As we get closer to the date, I'll let you know my schedule while I'm there. I'll be in touch. Chief Ted Langdon.

Wow, that was great! He was coming here, so I didn't need to figure out how to get to Danbury. When I told Emily about my message from Chief Langdon, she said, "I think my dad's going to that conference. It's downtown at the Convention Center. Maybe he could bring you there."

That sounded like a plan. I was sure her father would want a complete explanation for why I was meeting with Chief Langdon. I waited a little before I asked him to help me get downtown to meet the chief just because I wasn't ready and wanted to develop my explanation. I was sure it would get back to my father, so I'd need to prepare for that, too. I asked Emily to wait before saying anything to her dad about Chief Langdon. I wanted to be the one to ask. I was sure that he'd mention it to my father or my grandfather. By that time, I wanted to have my explanation for the meeting ready for everyone. Maybe it would be easier to take the bus.

Chapter 19

Halloween had finally arrived! This was close to my favorite holiday. I remember planning my costume for months when I was a kid and poor Grandma, who made my costume every year, made a trip to the store to get the fabric and supplies for whatever I had planned to wear. One year I was a bumblebee. Grandma made the costume out of black and yellow fur in alternating stripes. After I put it on, we stuffed it with newspapers to make it look puffy. I wore black tights, black shoes, and we made antennas out of pipe cleaners and black pom-poms. I think that was my favorite costume of all of them. Some were easier, like a princess. I wore a fancy satin dress that Grandma bought at Goodwill, and we made a crown out of some old broken jewelry. Grandma put as much effort into making the costumes as I did into planning what I would be, maybe more.

This year my friends and I were too old to trick or treat, but we wanted to be out on Halloween, so a group of about ten of us went to the local children's hospital to distribute stuff to the kids who were there. Em's mother made the arrangements. Candy wasn't always good for these kids, so we got some toys from our local toy fund. We asked the staff to turn down the lights, and we put on silly hats and carried plastic pumpkins lit with battery-operated candles through the pediatric floor as we gave out the toys. We stayed and talked to the kids and played a few games and left a pumpkin on each nightstand for them to keep. Some of their parents were there too, and one mother gave me a hug and thanked us for coming. When she finished hugging me, I looked at her face and she had tears in her eyes. I got a little weepy myself because I thought about my mother and how touched she'd be to see us there making other kids happy, especially because she worked with kids with problems when she was a speech pathologist.

Afterwards, we went to Jodi's house for pizza. We sat around playing music and talking about the kids. Some were very sick, while others were getting ready to go home. They said some funny things to us and seemed to have a lot of fun even though most were probably not feeling very well. We left them smiling, which made us feel great about visiting them. We talked about how lucky we were to be healthy and how sad we felt for the kids who might not recover. It was an unconventional Halloween for us.

Word had gotten around about our road trip, and as we ate our pizza, our friends asked about the colleges we saw and what we liked and didn't like about them. Jodi, Nicole, and Emily talked about colleges. Then, somehow, Emily slipped in that she had met Jake in Danbury. The questions flew.

"Did you meet him when you visited the college?"

"Is he going there?"

"What year is he in?"

"Did the rest of you meet him?"

Emily answered carefully so she wouldn't give away that he lived next door to 43 Windthorne, my family's old house, because then we'd get into a million questions about my mother's death, and this had been such a nice evening that I didn't want to bring up that topic or answer questions about it. My friends closed ranks around me to protect me from all the questions.

"Jake was here this weekend to look at the University," Emily said, "but he really wants to go to UConn, so I don't think he'll be back."

"I thought you said you met him at the college in Danbury."

"We went to a concert, and he was there," said Em. "He lives in Danbury and a lot of the high school kids in the area go to the concerts at the college."

That seemed to satisfy everyone. I realized how much support my friends were to me and how close we had become on our road trip. I thought about how they had shared their scariest moments, how much we trusted each other. The three of them are the best.

The next day, I got up and put on my old clothes. I loved how yoga pants just slipped right on, no zippers or buttons. And I also loved the feel of my old sweatshirt. It had my school's name on the front and I'd had it for the four years I'd been there. It used to be navy blue when I first got it, but it faded. Now it was very soft and cozy and warm. I needed to be warm because today I was planning to spend time in the attic looking through the boxes up there for anything to do with my mother.

I went downstairs for breakfast. Grandma had just returned from her walk with her rosy cheeks and her hair all messy from the wind.

"Hi Mari," she said. "How was your Halloween celebration?"

"Grandma, it was great. The kids loved it, and their parents enjoyed it too. It felt so good to do what we did, to do something good for other people. I think Mom would be proud."

"Well, I'm proud of you if that counts for anything."

"It counts, Grandma."

Was I spending so much time trying to look for my mother's killer that I was neglecting Grandma? That made me feel sad, because she had done so much for me, being a substitute mother to me for all this time. The bumble bee costume stuck in my memory as a kind of symbol of how much I meant to her and how much she meant to me.

"Grandma, remember when you made me that bumble bee costume?"

"How could I forget? You were the cutest bumble bee ever."

Her eyes lit up, and she got an enormous smile across her face. "I'll bet that somewhere in the attic there's a picture of you in that costume."

"I'll look for it while I'm up there today."

And at that moment, the smile on her face disappeared. "What are you looking for?" she said.

"I'm not sure. Pictures, letters, books. Maybe some videos. Remember how I wanted to find a video of Mom? Maybe there's some stuff packed away up there."

"I'm not sure there's much up there. We didn't bring much from Connecticut, and we threw away a lot of stuff years ago." Her voice had become very quiet, and she looked away from me."

"Well, I'll look just in case." I headed upstairs to the entrance to the attic. Since it was Fall, the attic was chilly, so I was thankful for my sweatshirt. The attic had a particular smell, kind of musty and dusty at the same time. I switched on the light and saw stacks of boxes, an old trunk, a bookcase, two wooden chairs and a small table in front of thc window. There were cobwebs that made walking around creepy. There were labels on each of the boxes in marker. I recognized Grandma's writing on most of them; a few were in my dad's writing and a couple were in a third handwriting which might have been my mother's. I'd need to go through the boxes one by one. I stood by the window and took a box and put it on the table and opened it. As I reached into the box, I heard a noise coming from outside. What was that? Thuds and clunks coming from the backyard.

I looked out the window and saw Grandma out by the woodpile. She had an ax in her hands and was chopping wood. She picked up a log, stood it up, raised the ax high over her head and brought it down with all her strength. The log split cleanly in half. She continued at a fast pace. Stand the log upright, raise the ax high, chop; stand the log, raise the ax high, chop. The ax came down violently. Thud, then clunk. Thud as the ax hit the log and split the wood, then clunk as the split logs fell to the ground.

As the wood pieces fell, she reached down to pick them up and threw them aside. All her movements were deliberate and fast. She looked angry. Her hair came loose from her ponytail and hung in front of her face as she worked. She pushed strands of it back over her ears.

I watched, and I felt my heartbeat speed up. My chest tightened and I couldn't breathe. What was Grandma doing? I knew she was chopping wood, but it seemed like more than that. Suddenly it felt as if I had been punched hard in the stomach, or I had a fist caught in my throat. As I watched her chop I wondered, with this horrible feeling, if Grandma had killed my mother. She had the strength and knew how to use an ax, but why would she do it? It couldn't be...or could it?

As horrified as I was, I could not take my eyes off Grandma and as much as I wanted to look away, I couldn't. I was trembling.

I sat down and tried to think, but I couldn't concentrate. Why would she? How could she? Did she? But Brenda said she left Danbury the day before they killed Mom. She couldn't have. But she could have if she wanted to and planned to. Grandma was a very determined woman.

Feeling stunned by what I had just seen, thought, and imagined, I couldn't move from that chair. Now what would I do? I couldn't say anything to her. Should I call the police? On my own grandmother? Why? It was just what I thought and not backed up with proof. At that point, I stayed quiet about what I saw. I sat upright in the chair. I looked at the stack of boxes in front of me, hoping to find clues, but afraid of the clues I might find and how much they could hurt.

The boxes were coated with dust. The one I chose first was also sealed with packing tape. I had brought some scissors with me and despite my hands shaking because of what I had seen from the attic window, I used them to slit it open. I found a bunch of office supplies, a stapler, ruler, hole puncher, a desk calendar, memo pads. Nothing too important...wait! I took out the desk calendar and saw it was from the year my mother died. It was one of those calendars that looked like a little loose-leaf book mounted on a plastic platform. I turned to February and the day they killed her. The page was missing. Also missing were two pages before and the pages from the next two weeks. There were appointments listed from January 1 until the days that were missing. There were no appointments listed in the rest of the book. Whose calendar was it? I put it aside to look at later.

I texted Emily and asked her to come and help me. I just needed her company. I was still trembling, still shaken up by seeing my grandmother from the attic window. Em arrived about fifteen minutes later and I felt relieved to hear her footsteps on the stairs.

"Em, thanks for coming. I hope you are wearing your old clothes. It's so dusty up here."

Em sneezed. "I guess so! What do you need me for?"

A lot more than I was ready to tell her. I lifted one box to the table and slit it open. It was the box labeled with what I thought was my mother's handwriting.

"Look in here and see if you can find anything important."

"Like what?" she asked.

"Something important to my mother or something about her. You're just going to have to guess when you see something. If you aren't sure, ask me."

The box we opened was full of baby clothes.

"These must have been yours, Mari. They're all pink and frilly. The sizes would have been too small for you when your mother died. Your mother probably put them in the box when you outgrew them. My mother has some boxes like this. Some clothes belonged to my brother and some to me."

"Now that could be something important, Em! You're right. My mother would have packed them away. She probably was hoping to save them in case she had another baby. Let's look through the clothes one piece at a time. We might find something."

"Really, Mari? One piece at a time? You'll miss going off to college."

"Hilarious, Emily. This is too important to joke about."

We took everything out of the box, unfolded each item, held it up and looked at it. The outfits were all cute and very frilly, definitely for a baby girl. But in the box's bottom was a pink book titled *Baby's First Year*. It looked like a record that my mother had kept of me. I looked through it and saw her handwriting. I showed Emily, but I wanted to take it somewhere private and read it by myself, reminding me of a monkey I had seen in a cage at the zoo. It found a banana and took it off to a corner and faced the wall to eat by itself and protect the banana from the others. That's how I felt about the baby book. Also in the box was a small silver bell on a heavy plastic pink ring. I think it was a teething ring. The bell was flat and engraved on one side with a very fancy "M" and on the other side, the Roman numbers XLIII. The same number was on my locket. I took both the book and the bell and set them aside.

"Look at this, Em. My teething ring! Look at the engraving. XLIII, just like my locket."

"This really was an important number to your mother. You need to find out why. It's an important clue."

"Em," I said, "I'll put this away for later. Let's just keep going with the rest of these boxes."

Em put the next box on the table. It had my grandmother's writing on the side and was heavier than the first. We opened it and found some photo albums.

"These have to be important, Mari," Em said, almost whispering.

I turned the pages of the first one. It looked like an album of pictures totally of my dad. There he was as a newborn with Grandma and Grandpa coming home from the hospital, then some pictures of his christening, and toddler pictures. Funny how much he looked like himself today, even with that quiet, frowning face that he made so often when I asked him about Mom. The album went up to college with pictures of his graduation. Then that album ended.

"Hey Em, I wonder if there is one in here of my mother?" We

lifted the albums out to see what the subjects were. There was an ancient album. We took it out and opened it. It looked like antique pictures, and I wondered whose parents and family they were. Next was a pink album of baby pictures, –mine. I was a tiny newborn, and then a toddler, preschooler, up to about age 12. And there was a picture of me in the bumble bee costume. This album was a lot like the one of my dad. Maybe Mom started it, but looking at how many years it covered, I knew it had to have been put together by either my grandmother or my dad.

"You were so cute," Emily said. "What happened?"

"Hilarious, Em."

As we looked at the pictures in my album, Em said, "Hey Mari, look at the pictures. They're just pictures of you. No pictures of your mother or father or anyone else. Isn't that kind of strange?"

I wasn't sure.

I put the album aside with the baby book and the bell.

Then my phone buzzed. A text from Brenda. *Hi Mari. How's everything?*

I had no desire to text with her, but I figured if I didn't get back, the next thing would be a call. *Everything's good, thanks.* And then I turned off the phone.

Over the next few days, Em and I went through some more boxes. Old Christmas ornaments, some toys, but nothing that seemed important. There were still a few more boxes, but we stopped our attic search for now.

"I don't think there's anything important here," Emily said.

"I'm not so sure," I said. "But we can stop if you promise to help me again."

"Sure," she said. "I'm really stuck in this now. Whatever you need."

Chapter 20

Snow fell early in Rochester this year. Most of my friends skied or snowboarded. Me, I liked to stay inside, drink hot cocoa and read a book. If my friends organized something like sledding or building a snowman, I'd go, but I couldn't wait to get home where it was warm. Today we had a big snowstorm, and it was heavy enough to close the schools. I went to my room to write in my journal. I needed to process seeing my grandmother chopping wood in the yard. I had such a powerful, physical reaction to it, and I knew I had to translate it into slow motion to watch it closely and analyze my reaction. I opened the journal and looked at what I had last written– the reasons someone would murder another person– and I applied them to what I knew about the relationship between my mother and my grandmother.

Revenge. If Grandma killed her, what did my mother do that made Grandma want to kill her?

Anger. There had to be such intense anger to inspire murder. Not the anger you'd feel if somebody forgot to return a borrowed sweater. It needed to be much bigger than that.

Jealousy. Of what? What did Mom have that Grandma didn't? Well, Mom had Dad and me. Would that do it? I put this one aside for later.

Hatred. Would Grandma hate Mom? Why? I think if you hated

somebody a lot it might just grow bigger inside you every day until you must do something about it. I never heard her say bad stuff about my mother, at least not in front of me, but now that my mother is gone, there would be no need to. Again, I put that aside.

Accident. This was no accident. It was a vicious murder.

To save another person. Yes, but nobody was in danger. Wait a minute. Maybe Grandma felt like I was in danger, or maybe Dad was in danger. But what kind of danger? Did she think Mom would hurt us? Why and how?

In war. No war here. Uh-oh, maybe there was a war in the family. But Mom had no family. If there was a war, it would've needed to be between Mom and Dad or Mom and Grandma.

If you were crazy. Grandma didn't seem crazy, but she sure looked upset while she was chopping wood.

To stop someone from doing something. What would Mom have been doing that Grandma needed to stop? Breathing came to mind.

Self-defense. Did Mom start it first? I doubt it. Mom was asleep when the murder happened unless it was a holdover from the night before. Could be.

"Oh come on, Mom, "I said. "Help me out." And I held on to my locket.

As if in a daze, I put down my journal and I walked upstairs to the attic to continue searching through the boxes. I opened another box. This one was full of pictures in frames. One of my parents on their wedding day, one of me sitting in a pretty chair in a pink dress next to a big white "1." Probably taken in a photo studio to celebrate my first birthday. Another frame had a certificate, not a picture. It said, "Certificate of Marriage." A record of my parents' marriage. I looked at their names and then at the date, February, in the same year I was born. But my birthday was in September, so that meant that my mother was pregnant when they got married. This was the second jolt in one day. I just sat in that chair in the attic, frozen in place, and then Grandma called up the stairs to me, "Mari, I made some soup. Would you like some?"

What would I do now? What I had seen out the window still upset me, and the date of my parents' wedding left me speechless. I had to make a conscious decision to pull myself together, to be in the kitchen with Grandma without losing it. I took some deep breaths, closed my eyes, and answered her.

"Sure Grandma. I'll be right down."

"What are you doing up there?" she asked.

"Oh, just going through some more boxes."

I sat at the kitchen table and ate my soup. Grandma was moving around the kitchen cleaning up after the soup making. She had her back to me as she wiped down the stove. I started a conversation. "Grandma, did you and Mom get along?" She stopped moving and continued to stand with her back to me.

"I guess so, Mari. No worse than other mothers-in-law and daughters-in-law."

"What do you mean, 'no worse?'" I went on.

"We had our disagreements from time to time."

"Like?"

"I wished you all lived closer, for one."

"But we lived in Danbury because of Dad's job. That wasn't Mom's idea. That's where the job was."

"You're right, I guess. Maybe the disagreement was more with your dad."

"Did you like my mother, Grandma?"

"I had to. She was your dad's wife and your mother."

"Had to? It sounded like you were being forced."

"I was. Lots of mothers-in-law disagree with their daughters-in-law. You both love the same man. It's for different reasons, but I guess there's some jealousy there, especially when the man chooses his wife over his mother."

There it was, that word from my list, "jealousy."

"But Grandma, isn't the man supposed to choose his wife over his mother?"

She turned to face me. "I didn't always agree with his choices."

"Besides the move to Danbury, what other choices?"

"Getting married. I thought your parents were too young to get married. Grandpa and I thought your dad's career was more important, that he needed to concentrate on that for a while. But your parents were in love and there were 'circumstances.'"

"I know about the circumstances," I said. "I found their marriage certificate."

She sat down at the table across from me and said, "So you know that she was pregnant before they were married."

I swallowed hard. Is that where the saying, "that was hard for me to swallow" originated? "I figured it out."

"She was alone except for your father. Her parents had passed away a few years before, so she had no support from her family. They both wanted to have you, so they got married. Your father got an offer for an excellent job, but it was in Connecticut. He wanted that job, so they left Rochester and moved to Danbury. We weren't happy with this situation at all. Your mother was not happy with us, and they rarely visited. She said it was hard to travel with a young baby. Although I knew that was true, I never totally bought it. But we visited about once a month to spend time with you."

"Did you stay at 43 Windthorne with us?" I asked.

"Yes, we did. We usually planned the visits on three-day weekends because both Grandpa and I had jobs, but if there was no holiday, we took our vacation time."

"Wow, Grandma, I never knew." I got up, and she stood up, too. I went over to her and gave her an enormous hug. "I'm so, so sorry."

"Why are you sorry, Mari? You did nothing wrong."

I had nothing more to say, except "Thanks for the soup." I left her and went back upstairs.

For me, this required an entry in my diary because it was such important news. It isn't every day that you find out that your mother was pregnant with you before she was married. A pregnancy is a life-changer. Dad was a responsible person, and he would not leave

Mom to take care of me by herself. But it sounded to me like Mom and Grandma never got along.

Dad came home. I knew he stopped to talk to Grandma. He always did. A few minutes later, I heard him coming up the stairs to change his clothes. His footsteps stopped outside my door and I heard a knock.

"Mari, talk to me."

"About what?"

The door opened, and he came in and sat in my chair. "Grandma said you and she talked today. Are you okay with what she told you about your mother and me?"

"There's nothing I can do about it, Dad, so yes, I guess I'm okay. It was such a surprise. Why didn't you tell me before?"

"I didn't think there was reason to."

"It's my life, Dad," I said, "So it's important to me. Is there anything else I need to know?"

"I don't think so, Mari."

"If there is," I said, standing up, "you need to tell me." I was annoyed at him for not telling me about my birth. I wanted him to know how upset I was.

"I will," he said. He nodded and left the room.

Finally, I was getting some facts about my life and my mother's life that might relate to her murder. I opened the diary and wrote:

> *Dear Mom,*
>
> *I just was told one of the family's secrets, although I am not sure why it was such a secret. Lots of women get pregnant and aren't married. I don't think it's a big deal. Maybe it was a secret because you and Dad went ahead with the wedding, even though Grandma and Grandpa opposed the marriage. I think you were strong to do that. I'm sorry it hurt Grandma and Grandpa, but it was your life. I hope this didn't cause your murder.*
>
> *Love, Mari*

I sat there and thought about what I learned. How scared I

was when I saw Grandma with the ax; the history of my mother and my grandmother; my mother's stress of being pregnant and deciding to get married and leave Rochester. From what Grandma told me, it sounded like there might have been a lot of anger, or at least resentment about everything. I wondered what words they exchanged, and what they'd said each time they visited. I wasn't sure I wanted to find out. And then my phone buzzed with a text from Brenda.

Everything OK?" she wrote.

I sent her a thumbs-up.

Chapter 21

Em, Jodi, Nicole and I took a trip to the mall to hang out and do some Christmas shopping. We went to our favorite coffee place to sit and talk.

Emily said, "Guess who's coming home from school?"

"Seth?" I asked with a smile. "How come?"

"He's finishing early because he has no finals in two of his classes, so he'll be back the weekend before the holiday. What are you doing for Thanksgiving?" she asked the group.

"The usual," I said. You know we don't have any other family to visit."

Jodi answered, "We're staying here, and my dad's family is coming. My grandparents will be here, and my aunts are helping my mom cook. There will be a little Mexican food along with the turkey."

Nicole said, "We're going to Pennsylvania to visit friends of my parents. They live on a farm and when we go there, it feels like an old-fashioned Thanksgiving like from *Little House on the Prairie.* They even have a sheep, a cow, and a few chickens."

"Sounds like you should wear a Pilgrim outfit! Do you have those shoes with buckles on them?"

Now we were getting silly.

Then Emily said, "Mari, maybe you can come over after Seth

gets home. I know he'd like to see you. The three of us could go hiking in the woods together, and I'll bring the dog."

"Em, how about if you and the dog stay home and Seth and I go for a walk in the woods alone?"

"Woooo!" the three of them said simultaneously. "Sounds serious!"

"Are you going to carve your names in a tree?" Jodi asked.

"Or make a heart shape out of rocks?" Nicole said.

Seth was so nice. Because I had known both him and Emily since I was little, I knew a lot about him. He was a great guy, a wonderful friend, and I had always had feelings for him. I'd just have to see how it went.

"Are you having any company for Thanksgiving, Emily?" Nicole asked.

"We are." Em looked at me and said, "Jake and his mother are coming."

It didn't surprise me that Jake was invited, but it surprised me that Em's parents invited Brenda, Jake's mother.

"Wow, Em, Brenda, too?"

"Yeah. I invited Jake, but he worried about his mother spending the holiday alone, and you know my mom. If she thinks someone will be alone, she'll invite them, too. So, she did. They'll be here on Wednesday."

"Are they staying at your house?"

"No. Brenda insisted on a hotel. Besides, with my brother home, there's no room for them to stay with us."

As if on cue, I got an incoming text from Brenda. *Hi Mari. Great news! Jake and I will be in Rochester for Thanksgiving with Emily and her family. Looking forward to seeing you when we are in town.*

I sent her a thumbs up.

Seth traveled from Boston by Amtrak. Em's dad picked him up at the train station, and not that I planned it, but I was there when he got home. I was waiting for Emily in the living room. She was upstairs changing her clothes.

"Wow," he said. "It's so good to be home. Hi Mari. Where's Em?"

"Hi Seth," I smiled. "She's upstairs. How was the trip?"

"Long, but I don't mind. It gives me time to catch up on my sleep, relax and read. For me, it's almost like a vacation. Sometimes I meet interesting people, too. Today I traveled with one girl from school who was going home to Albany, so we got to talk a little. How are you doing?"

"I'm good. Your sister and I have been busy cleaning out my grandparents' attic."

"Did you find anything good? Buried treasure or valuable antiques, maybe?"

"So far just pictures. I'm looking for old videos of my mother, and stuff that belonged to her."

"I guess it's still hard for you, not having her and not knowing who killed her," he said.

I didn't know what to say. It was the first time I heard the concern in his voice. I looked up into his eyes and felt tears coming from mine.

"I'm sorry I got you upset," he said.

He put his arm around my shoulder and stood next to me until I pulled myself together. I went to the bathroom to wash my face. When I came back, Em was there.

"What's going on with you two?" she asked. She could see how red my eyes were, but the tears had dried, and I was pretty much back to normal.

"So, Seth," I said, "I heard your family is having guests for Thanksgiving. Then you get to meet Jake and his mother."

I was interested in finding out his impressions of both of them, but I'd just have to wait until Thanksgiving. Also, I was more interested in my upcoming meeting with Chief Langdon the week after.

Brenda and Jake arrived on Wednesday night. Brenda stayed at the hotel, but Jake came right over to Emily's house. Her parents, who are probably the nicest people in the world, were very glad to see him. I was too because he is a nice guy, and he makes Emily very happy.

"Mari, how's it going?" I wasn't sure whether he meant specifically about my mother's murder.

"It's going," I said.

"Jake let's take Max for a walk," said Em.

She leashed up the dog, and she and Jake took him out. Max liked Jake, too, but he was always tired when Jake was around because Emily and Jake took him for lots of walks so they could be alone. I went home to find out what I needed to do to help with Thanksgiving dinner.

"Grandma, what do you need me to do?" I asked.

"There isn't much, Mari. We're planning to go to the soup kitchen around noon to serve dinner to the homeless people there. Are you coming with us?"

"Of course." I loved doing that every year. I thought we should do it more often. Once a year wasn't enough.

"What can I do to help with our dinner?"

"Nothing, really. We had an invitation from Emily's parents to join them. I made apple and pumpkin pies to bring, so we'll be going there after the soup kitchen."

That was news to me, but great! That would give me more time to be around Seth, and I could monitor Brenda.

We went to the soup kitchen early and helped set up the steam tables. People started arriving at 11:30, even though the soup kitchen wasn't open until noon. They lined up outside the door. It was a chilly morning, and there was snow on the ground, so I'm sure the people wanted to be someplace warm and needed a hot meal. The soup kitchen was full of Thanksgiving smells, turkey, sweet potatoes, stuffing, gravy, and the ever-present pies and hot coffee. We opened the doors early because none of us wanted these people to stay out in the cold. It just wasn't right.

I watched as everyone came in. There were adults, but also there were families with children. I was glad that we could help. I thought about my parents. I was lucky to have had them and despite the murder of my mother; I was grateful for the life I had.

Chapter 22

"Happy Thanksgiving!" Em's parents, the Reese's hugged us as we entered their home. Grandma delivered the pies to the kitchen, and Mr. Reese offered everyone mugs of mulled cider with a cinnamon stick. We all gathered in the family room where a fire blazed in the fireplace. Brenda came over to give me a hug and she shook hands with my dad and grandparents.

Grandma extended her hand slowly. "Hi Brenda," she said. "It's good to see you again." She said it, but I could hear a little coldness in her voice.

"You too, Carol," Brenda replied.

I can't say they shook hands, more like they slid their palms together and removed them. They had stony expressions on their faces. No genuine affection there. Not that I expected any. Em and Seth's parents, being superb hosts, knew how to keep the conversation going without it erupting.

"Let's move into the dining room," Mrs. Reese said. "And could I get some help to bring out the food?"

"Sure, Mom." Seth and Emily got up and headed toward the kitchen.

The meal was delicious, and the conversation flowed. Most of it came from Seth, Em, Jake, and me, so there was a lot of laughing. The adults looked on, with Em's parents smiling and thoroughly enjoying the event. It was a long, relaxed dinner and after eating the pies that Grandma made, everybody pitched in to clean up and wash the dishes. The parents moved into the family room for coffee.

"Let's take the dog for a walk," Seth said. Poor Max. Another walk. All four of us put on our coats, Emily leashed up Max, and we headed out into the neighborhood. I could smell the wood fires burning in each house's fireplace, and there still was a hint of the smell of turkey in the air. Jake, Em and Max split off from Seth and me. I watched as Jake took the leash with one hand and put his other arm around Emily. And as I watched them, Seth took my hand. Despite everything, this was the best Thanksgiving ever.

When we got back, the party was ending. My family was on their way out the door. Brenda was still on the couch in the family room waiting for Jake. I thanked the Reeses for a wonderful time, and Seth, who was still holding my hand, offered to walk me home. We strolled together through the snow and fallen leaves and then, when we got to my house, Seth leaned toward me and said, "Do you mind if I kiss you?" I didn't mind at all. I turned my face up toward his and he kissed me gently on the lips.

"Good night, Seth," I said.

"Good night, Mari. Happy Thanksgiving."

"Yes, it was," I thought. And I went inside. When I got upstairs, I reached for my journal. Mom needed to know this. I touched my locket as I wrote:

Dear Mom,

Today is Thanksgiving, and I realized how much I am thankful for. For you and Dad, Grandma and Grandpa, my friends, my home and about a million other things. I guess I could say I am thankful for my life.

I think tonight was special too, because of Seth. We will see where that goes, but I like him a lot and he seems to like me enough to kiss me.

I am looking forward to the rest of the weekend. I am the happiest I have been in a long time. I just miss you very much. Love and Happy Thanksgiving, Mari.

Chapter 23

The next morning, I got a text from Brenda. *Hi Mari. Can we get together today?*

I called her back. "Hi Brenda. I want to check with Grandma but maybe you can come over and I can show you some stuff I found in the attic."

"Stuff that belonged to your mother?"

"Yeah. Some of it did. Maybe you can give me a hand going through it."

"Sure," she said. "I'd love to see what you found."

When I told Grandma that Brenda was coming, she seemed annoyed. More and more I was noticing Grandma's tension. When Brenda came into the room, Grandma's face tightened up. Her voice became unfriendly. I think she wanted to say, "I don't want that woman in my house!" but she let her in anyway.

Brenda arrived with Jake, who went directly over to Emily's house, and then she and I went upstairs to the attic. I showed her the boxes Em and I had set aside, the ones with things that seemed important to me. She went through the box of baby clothes and pulled out a very frilly dress.

"I bought this one for you for your first birthday," she said, smiling with a look of remembrance on her face.

She also recognized the baby book. "Have you read this yet?"

"No, I put it aside for later. I'm just sorting stuff now and then I thought I'd do a marathon of reading and going through pictures."

"I can't believe you haven't read it," she said. She sounded like she was scolding me. "I thought you were in such a big hurry to find out who murdered your mother."

I got angry, and I snapped at her. "Listen, Brenda. I'm doing this my way. I know you want to help, but I need you to back off. I need you to help me look through this stuff, but I don't want you to tell me how to do it. Anyway, I doubt that the name of her murderer is in a baby book."

She backed off. If I was her, I would have stormed out, but she didn't. Then I wondered why. She seemed to be looking for something, but what? I asked her a question that might lead to an important answer.

"Brenda, what happened to your husband?"

She had been carrying another box over to the table and froze.

"I told you; he left the year after your mother died. I don't know where he went. Like I said before, he just disappeared and left me on my own with Jake."

"Why did he go? Did you have a fight or something?"

"No. Why do you need to know about him?"

"Because he was around when my mother was killed. Maybe he did it. Maybe that's why he ran off."

"Look, I don't know why he left. He just disappeared. No call, no note. He went to work one day, and he didn't come home. I reported it to the police. They looked for him, but there was nothing. We tried to look for him on the internet. Again, nothing. He never showed up again at work. He didn't take a suitcase or clothes with him. Maybe he was having an affair, or maybe he had another family somewhere, or maybe he murdered your mother. I don't know. He might even be dead."

"You must be mad at him."

"You're darn right, I'm mad. He left me with a baby, a mortgage, no child support, no note, no reason. I'm angry. He hurt us very much. You can't imagine what it was like."

"I think I can." I felt tears coming on. "Somebody took my mother away. I'm angry too, but I'll find the person who did this to her and to me and my dad so they can pay for this."

"I need to leave." Brenda grabbed her coat. The hood caught on a nail and ripped, adding one more thing that upset her. She hurried down the stairs and out the front door to her car. I watched from the front attic window as she got in the car and made a call. Jake came out of Em's house, went to the car, and said something to her. Then she left and Jake went back to the house.

Now what? I needed to talk to Jake, so I flew down the stairs and over to Em's house. Jake and Em were in the kitchen.

"Jake, where did your mother go?"

"I'm not sure. But she was upset. She probably went back to the hotel to cool off. What happened at your house that got her so crazy?"

"I asked her about your father, Jake. I have questions about him."

"I guess she didn't like your questions."

"No, and she didn't answer any of them. She says he left for work and never came back. She's furious at him for that."

Em said, "Well, can you blame her? I'd be mad, too."

"Look, guys, I think Jake's dad might have some information about my mother's murder. He was around then. Maybe he saw something, or maybe he has some suspicions that should be investigated."

Jake said, "Mari, don't you think the police talked to him after the murder?"

"Sure, but maybe they missed something. And now he's missing and there's no way to follow up."

"But he left a year after the murder. By then, don't you think the investigation would have slowed down?"

"I don't know," I said. "But when I meet with Chief Langdon, you can bet that I'll ask him."

Em asked, "When are you meeting with him?"

"He's coming to town for a Law Enforcement Conference next week. He agreed to meet with me then."

"Do you want us to go with you?"

"No," I said. "I need to go alone."

I went back home, and I got a text from Emily telling me that Jake and Brenda were leaving tomorrow. I guess Brenda had had enough. Then I got a text from Jake.

Mari, can we get together before I leave tomorrow? I need to talk with you about my dad.

We set up a time to meet at the local coffee shop in the morning.

Chapter 24

Because of the holiday, the coffee shop was deserted. It smelled of early morning freshly brewed coffee. Jake and I sat in the back of the shop at a corner table and after our coffee arrived, Jake became silent. He looked down at his coffee mug and then raised his eyes toward my face.

"Mari, I need to tell you something important. Can you keep it a secret?"

"Of course. You can trust me. What's going on?"

"OK," he said, "I trust you, but you can't tell anyone, not even Emily. Promise me!"

Not even Emily? There was an urgent sound in his voice. I promised again, raising my right hand as if I was being sworn into a very important position. And I was. I was being sworn into an additional level of friendship, of trust. Jake stared at me and leaned forward, emphasizing the importance of what he was about to tell me.

"My dad is alive," he said. "I've been in touch with him many times in the past couple of years. I've wanted to tell you ever since the first day you came to Danbury and you started talking about your mother with me."

"So, your mother doesn't know?"

"No, and you can't tell her, and you can't tell Emily or anybody else," he said.

"How did you find him? Where has he been?"

I started talking in a whisper so no one would hear us, even though there was nobody around. Now I was leaning forward too. The coffee shop was empty except for the guy behind the counter who was busy filling glass canisters with fresh coffee beans. A noisy job, for sure, but it kept him from hearing what we were talking about.

Jake went on. "When he left, he went as far away as he could. He wound up traveling to Vancouver, Canada by train, where he got a job on a Canadian fishing boat that traveled up the coast toward Alaska. He wanted to disappear."

"But why?" I asked.

"I'm not sure, Mari. Maybe it had something to do with the murder, but he swore to me he didn't do it, and I believe him."

"So how do you communicate with him?"

"I use a burner phone and we text or use Facetime. My mother can't find out."

"How did you find him?' I asked.

"It was weird. He wanted to see what I was doing, so he found my school newspaper on-line. We were having a fundraiser for a local kids' program and my text number appeared in an article looking for volunteers. He texted me and told me to get a burner phone so calls and texts couldn't be traced from my phone and gave me his number. I called him and we talked for a long time. He said back then he needed to leave Danbury and leave us for his own reasons. He didn't want to discuss them. Crazy, isn't it?"

"Wow. It sure is crazy. How often do you talk to him?"

"Every couple of weeks. No special day, but he times it so I get the call in the afternoon while my mother is at work so she won't find out."

"Do you know where he is?" I asked.

"He hasn't told me. I asked him, but he doesn't want to tell me."

"Why not? Something's not right about this, Jake. I guess we knew that, but what's going on? I really need to talk to him," I said. "I've got so many questions to ask him. Why did he disappear? What does he know about my mother's murder?"

"I know, Mari. I know how desperate you are for information. I was feeling a lot of what you're feeling now. I almost went crazy wondering what happened to my father and why he left, just like I know you're going crazy now wondering why someone murdered your mother. At least I know now that my dad is okay. Look, I'll talk to him some more and see if I can work something out. I want to know where he is, too."

"Thanks, Jake. Thanks so much for telling me. I promise this is safe with me. I hope I can talk to your dad at some point. Maybe he's got some information that I can use. I sure hope so. Please tell him I need to talk to him. Can you do this for me?"

"I'll try. Listen, I need to go. My mother wants to leave, and I need to say goodbye to Em. I'll stay in touch with you, but I'll be using the burner phone."

He gave me the number for his second phone, and a hug. Then we walked to Em's house so he could say goodbye. Em was looking out the window as we arrived. She opened the door.

"Hi, you two. Where have you been?"

"I went out for a walk and coffee this morning and I ran into Jake," I said. "I brought him back to you so he could kiss you goodbye." I smiled at her, knowing she probably would ask me a million questions later.

I went home and went up to the attic.

Chapter 25

Despite the dust and cobwebs, the attic was becoming my special place, a quiet place where I could think and plan my search for Mom's murderer. My attention went to the rest of the boxes. I wondered who had packed them at 43 Windthorne. Who decided what got taken and what got thrown out or left behind, and why? I needed to ask Grandma. Somebody who knew my mother packed the boxes. Even if professional movers brought the stuff here, somebody had to have made those choices before the boxes were packed and put on the moving truck. Was there a pattern to what they packed? Mostly the things were sentimental, like the pictures and Christmas ornaments. The contents of the box with the baby clothes had to have been packed by Mom before she died, not long after my first birthday. Probably Grandma could tell me. I called down to her, "Grandma, could you come up here for a minute?"

I heard her footsteps on the stairs, and she came through the doorway with a serious look on her face. "What do you need?"

"Grandma, who packed these boxes at 43 Windthorne? Was it you?"

"I did some of it, but I believe your dad did most of it. Wait, the handwriting on the side of the box is your mother's. I guess she packed some boxes for storage. Your dad had to get things out of there before the house went on the market. He left the furniture and all the kitchen stuff. I guess that everything else got thrown away or donated to Goodwill. After he sold the house, he told the realtor to get rid of what he left, and I think he gave everything else away."

"Except my mother's rocking chair, right?"

"I guess so, but I don't understand why he left the chair behind. Maybe because it matched the room. Maybe it was too sentimental for him to keep."

"Grandma, I've never been to Mom's grave. I'd like to visit her. I know she's in the cemetery nearby. Can you tell me where her grave is?"

"Sure, but I'll go with you. We can go this afternoon. Put on your boots. I'm sure there's snow and some mud out there. I'll meet you downstairs when you're ready to go."

"Can we stop for some flowers, first?"

"Sure. We'll stop at the supermarket, and you can pick something up."

Boots, warm parka, wool hat, gloves. We got to the store, and I bought a single beautiful red rose. The clerk tied a red ribbon on the stem, added a sprig of baby's breath and put it in a cone-shaped bag. Perfect for my mother because it was so pretty, yet simple. I knew the cemetery only from driving by. I had never been inside, but it was very flat, and the snow blew over it and formed drifts. The wind was frigid and there were very few trees. It was not like an old-fashioned cemetery. There were no headstones, just grave markers that laid flat on the ground and the occasional tree. I really wished there were headstones. On the other side of town was an old cemetery full of angels and other statues. I wished they'd buried my mother in that other cemetery because it was so beautiful. I wanted her to have a statue of a Victorian angel as a headstone. I thought it would fit her better. Grandma drove to the cemetery, and we went down the narrow road to Section 7. She parked along the edge of the road.

"Her grave is in this row about halfway down, I think."

We got out of the car and walked down the row until we found the marker. It was a small, plain granite plaque. I brushed off the leaves and snow that had covered her name, Marianne Corelli Franklin, and the dates of her birth and murder. Standing there, looking down at the place where they buried her, I noticed that there was no room on either side of her grave for any other family members. No room for Dad or me or Grandma and Grandpa. It was a snowy day, and I hated the thought of her lying in that cold grave. I hated the thought of her lying there alone, forever. I knelt in the snow and put my hand on the ground where I imagined her head was. Holding on to her locket engraved with XLIII, I placed the rose on the marker too, and said a prayer that I would find the person who did this to her. As I got up, Grandma put her arm around my shoulder, and we walked back to the car.

"Why is Mom buried in a spot with no room for anyone else, like Dad or me next to her? That doesn't seem right. Don't people have family burial plots?"

"Yes, they do. I'm not sure why your dad picked this spot. I know we all wanted this to be over. And he buried her in a hurry. He bought the plot, and we had a simple funeral. He was upset; well, we all were, and maybe he wasn't thinking about it. I'm sure he didn't want to think about you dying, and he wasn't planning on dying himself because he knew you needed him."

Grandma seemed to patronize me or placate me so I wouldn't make a big deal about the gravesite. I kind of let it go at that point. I was glad to be here, to see where Mom's body was so I could come back to visit her by myself. When we got back to the house, I thanked my grandmother for taking me to the cemetery and climbed the stairs to the attic to resume my hunt for clues and to think.

Then my phone buzzed. I had a text from Brenda. Nothing important, just a *Hi. How's it going?*

I typed, *Fine* and turned off the phone.

Chapter 26

When I walked through the attic door, I put my hand on my locket and looked around. A few more unopened boxes sat waiting for me under the dusty rafters. I decided I needed a break. Our school psychologist had done a presentation about taking care of our mental health, and I remembered her telling us to take some time for relaxation and laughter. Today was very emotional, and I'd decided that the best thing for my mental health was to get together with my friends and do something fun. I texted the three of them and asked for some ideas, and immediately they texted back, "Let's go sledding!" Em and I used to do it every winter when we were little kids, and I remembered how much fun we had.

Near our neighborhood was a hill that was perfect for sledding. It was just the right height and in a good snowstorm the hill always got lots of snow. We brought our plastic sleds (mine was red and when I was about eight years old, I had written my name in big letters on it with a marker.) We were glad to see that there were not a lot of kids there. More space for us! We slid down the hill, rolled off the sleds, got covered in snow and laughed till we could barely stand up. Each time we came down faster and faster as our sleds packed the snow down and made it very slick. We needed to have a snowball fight, and I was the recipient of what felt like twenty snowballs hitting my body. I was laughing so hard I couldn't catch my breath, and I was too weak with laughter to throw any snowballs back, so I became an easy target. I needed that good laugh. I was lucky to have these girls in my life to laugh with. Today they sure helped my mental health.

Soon it got dark, and we walked home, still laughing, covered in snow, and dragging our sleds. Emily said, "We'd better get home before the streetlamps come on or we'll get into trouble." That brought back memories of when we were kids. That was the rule; home before the streetlamps came on.

After dinner I took a long, hot shower to warm up after a wintry afternoon in the snow. Because it was an emotional day and a lot of crazy sledding with my crazy friends, I went to bed early. I was so tired I couldn't even write in my journal. I got into bed and fell asleep quickly, not even remembering my head hitting the pillow, and I don't think my body moved at all during the night. That good night's sleep was another contribution to my mental health. The next day I texted Chief Langdon, just to check that he was still coming to Rochester for the police conference and to remind him he agreed to meet with me. There were only a few days left before he was due to arrive, and I needed to set up a time for us to get together.

Chapter 27

Hi Chief Langdon,

I hope you are still planning on coming to Rochester. My neighbor, Detective Reese from our local police department, is planning to be at the conference and he will take me downtown. Maybe we can meet in the hotel restaurant. Please let me know what a good day and time would be. I have lots of questions for you.

Mari Franklin

Once again, I spent the rest of the morning checking my phone looking for his text. My phone buzzed, and I knew it was from him.

Dear Mari,

Based on the schedule of the conference, I have some free time on Saturday morning at about 10:00. I hope that works for you. We can meet in the main lobby of the hotel. The restaurant sounds fine, but I'll check to see if there is a quieter place where we can meet. I am looking forward to our meeting. I hope the information I have will be helpful to you. Chief Langdon

I went over to Em's house and found her dad in the kitchen.

"Hi Mr. Reese. I need a favor."

"Sure, kiddo. But I think I know what you'll ask. Emily said you need a ride to the police conference. I can take you. I'll be there every day."

I was surprised that Emily had asked him for me even though I wanted to ask him myself.

"I only need a ride on Saturday morning to meet Chief Langdon, if that's okay."

"Sure," he said. "Can I help you otherwise? I've been in the police department for a long time. I need to tell you, though, that you should leave the police work to the police. This is dangerous stuff. After you meet with Chief Langdon, if you need input, remember that I'm here."

"Mr. Reese, who do you think killed my mother?" I asked.

"I do sometimes think about her murder, but I'd need more information to solve it. I don't know what the police have. I'm sure Chief Langdon could fill in some blanks for me. I could go to your meeting with him. It's up to you."

Mr. Reese was like a second dad to me. He's known me since I was three, after my mother was murdered and we came to Rochester. I appreciated his offer, but it was important for me to do this by myself.

"Thanks, Mr. Reese," I said. "I'll let you know."

"OK." he said. "I'll see you Saturday morning at 9:30." Then I went upstairs to find Emily and the dog.

Saturday couldn't come soon enough. At 9:30 sharp, I was ready to go with a notebook under my arm. The hotel was downtown and was used for a lot of conferences. By the time we drove downtown, parked, and walked from the garage to the lobby, it was 10:00 and there was Chief Langdon waiting for me. I headed toward him and shook hands. "Hi, Chief," I said. "I hope you had a pleasant trip."

Mr. Reese introduced himself to the chief. They exchanged some police talk and then Mr. Reese said, "Mari, when you're ready to go, text me."

Chief Langdon and I headed for the restaurant, and the hostess brought us to a quiet table in the back corner. He brought a leather case with him, and after we sat, he unzipped it and took out a manila file.

"Mari, listen. I've been working on your mother's murder case for a long time. I think some information I've got will upset you."

"Chief, your house was upsetting to me. Just being in the place where the murder took place was so weird. Seeing my room and Mom's rocking chair left me shaking inside. I've tried to figure out why somebody would murder her, and came up with a list of motives, like revenge, anger, jealousy, hatred. I also thought someone might kill to save another person, or if they were crazy."

"That was good logic," he said. "I've investigated a few murders, and I came to that list myself."

"And when you looked at the list, did you come up with a suspect?" I asked with caution. I was feeling torn between my impression of him being kind of odd because he lived in a murder house and wanting to work with him because he had spent so much effort on the case.

"I'm still working on it. That's why I wanted to meet with you. When you visited my house, I could see how important this was to you. You traveled all the way to Danbury to see the house in person. I could never have denied you the opportunity of a tour. It was your house long before it was mine."

"Could you tell me what you have in the other rooms?" I asked.

"One room is my bedroom, but the other room has all of my information about the murder. I have files and pictures, and a big whiteboard where I write questions that I need answered. I have a photo of your mother, another of your father, and a picture of you as a baby. I also have pictures of everyone who I think might be a person of interest."

Chief, this is major news! "Who?" I asked. "Who do you suspect?"

"I don't want to tell you yet. I want you to tell me what your suspicions are. When your mother was murdered people clammed up. Your dad took you and moved away. He wasn't easily available to me at all. Your grandparents weren't helpful. I interviewed the neighbors. Nothing there, and then Jake's dad disappeared."

"So, I guess you know nothing about what happened to Jake's dad."

"No," Chief Landon said, "Do you?"

"Not really," I lied. I looked away, remembering how I promised Jake that I wouldn't tell anyone what he had told me about his dad. "I'm just guessing, but the way he disappeared makes me wonder if maybe he was killed or maybe he knew something and is in witness protection. What do you think?"

"I think his family would have heard if he was killed, and unless there's some crime I've never heard about, I don't think he's in witness protection," he said. "He just might be great at hiding out. I don't know why he's gone any more than you do. We found no evidence that your mother's murder involved him, though."

"Can I ask you why you bought our house?"

"The price was right. Your dad wanted to sell it quickly, but it didn't sell at the original price, so he listed it at a lower price. As soon as the price dropped, I bought it through Greg Henderson, Jake's dad. He was a realtor."

"I didn't know that about Jake's dad. I knew about the price and everything, but I didn't know who the realtor was. It seems like every time I talk to someone about the murder, I find out another minor fact. It's like putting together a thousand-piece jigsaw puzzle. Did you buy it with all the furniture and other stuff left in the house?"

"I did. I wouldn't let them clean it out, even though the realtor was arranging for a clean-out service. I wanted any clue I could find. After I went through it, I donated the furniture, and had a housecleaner come to clean out what was left. Who else have you talked to?" he asked.

"Just those people close to my mother and close to the murder; my dad, my grandparents, Brenda and Jake and you, but every time I talk to someone else, I find out something new. Each conversation opens some additional facts. Plus, I've been going through the boxes my family brought from Danbury. They've been in the attic untouched for years."

"Have you found anything in them?"

"A few things that led to a few more things, but nothing tied to the murder."

"What does Jake know?" he asked.

"Not much, but the murder affected him, too. And who knows why his father left town? Jake's lost a parent, too. Except he's got hope that his dad is alive, while I know my mother is dead." I had to swallow hard when I said, "dead." The word itself was so final, like the thud of a casket hitting the ground.

Next Chief Langdon said, "I see you're wearing your mother's necklace with XLIII engraved on it. I remember it was part of the crime scene. What does the number signify? Do you know?"

"No, I don't," I said. "It originally belonged to my grandmother, my mother's mother. My Dad and Mom gave it to me for my eighteenth birthday. The number must have meant something, but I haven't figured it out yet."

"Your Mom?"

"Yes," I said, "Dad told me she always intended for me to have it."

"You know she was wearing it when she died, right?" Chief Langdon asked.

"Yeah. I think her spirit lives in it now."

"I think she lives in my house, too."

Of course she did. I saw her rocker moving.

"What makes you think she's there?" I asked.

"Sometimes I hear noises. I keep the door to the nursery closed. If I go in there, sometimes I think I see the rocking chair moving like someone is sitting in it. I also keep the door closed to the murder room. I don't like to go in there at all. You saw that I keep it empty. It's because it's always cold in there. It feels like a crypt."

"But if it's so weird in that house, you must have had another reason to buy it besides price," I said. "No matter how cheap the house was, I can't imagine living in a house that's that creepy."

"Mari, if you believed like I do, that what happens in the house is because of your mother's spirit that lives there, you might live there, too."

"I guess I might. Knowing it was her, I guess I would. But she's my mother. That's a powerful reason for me to connect to that house. I guess I'm asking you why you're so connected. You could just as easily have lived around the corner and investigated the murder."

"Not like this," he said. "I listen to her all the time. She talks to me. I can look in corners for clues that we missed, like hair or DNA."

"Then why is her bedroom painted red?" I asked. "You told me you couldn't get her blood out of the walls, so you painted them red, and then you replaced the wood floors."

"I wanted the reminder of what the room looked like when I first saw it. I didn't want to forget," he said. I could have left it as it was, but it was too harsh, even for me.

That image made me shudder. I realized it was weird that he painted the room red. It reminded me of that scary movie, *The Shining*, with the word REDRUM on the bedroom door.

"So, what have you found?" I asked. And at that point he opened the manila folder that he had brought.

I settled in and asked the server to bring me a cup of tea. The chief asked for decaf coffee. Then he told me what he found. "First off, nobody broke into the house through the basement. The windows are glass blocks. No one could get in that way. There were footprints outside in the snow and mud, so we know there was someone outside near the house." He showed me photographs of the footprints.

"Are they from a man or a woman?" I asked.

"Hard to tell. They're from plain heavy rubber boots; either a man or a woman could wear them."

"How did the murderer get into the house, then?" I asked. "Was there a break-in?"

Chief Langdon looked up from the papers in front of him and said, "No broken windows. No broken locks. So, either someone with access to the house got in, someone let the murderer in, or somebody forgot to lock the door."

"But why? Why would someone go into our house? Was it a robbery?"

"There was no evidence of robbery. Nothing was missing. The only furniture that they disturbed was in the bedroom where they killed your mother."

"What other reason could it be?" I asked.

"I thought maybe an attempt to kidnap you."

"Me? But I wasn't hurt, right? I wasn't kidnapped. I was in my crib when my father got home. What makes you think it was a kidnap attempt?" I hadn't even thought of that.

"Just a guess," he said.

"But if it was wet, snowy and muddy, weren't there footprints inside?" I asked.

"Interesting question," he said, "There were no footprints. The murderer must have slipped the boots off when he or she came in."

"What would make somebody do that, especially a murderer?" I asked.

"Well, you tell me what you think," he said.

"Maybe because walking in boots is noisy, and the person didn't want to wake up anyone in the house?"

"Anything else?"

"Maybe because it would be messy to leave the boots on?"

"You got it," he said.

"But Chief, if the person didn't want to make a mess, why use an ax? Why not use a gun, why not strangle her?"

Chief Langdon got quiet and then he said, "Mari, whoever did this was furious at your mother. I don't understand why or what the person was mad at, but that person was furious. I saw the room and the body, and I stand by the evidence."

I literally couldn't speak. His choice of words stunned me. Who could have been so angry and vicious enough to kill my mother with an ax, yet so careful that they took their boots off?

"They killed her and left blood all over the bed, so they must have gotten blood all over themselves. They went back to the boots, put them on, and left?" I continued, "What happened to the ax? And didn't they leave footprints inside between the bedroom and the door when they left?"

"They left the ax behind with your mother's body. I think they didn't take it because they didn't want to have to get rid of it after the police got involved. We have it with the other evidence from the murder. There wasn't much else. I think the murderer cleaned up and took whatever they used to clean with them. Don't forget they had a lot of time. They killed her early in the morning and nobody found her until your dad came home at about six o'clock. I think the murderer planned everything in advance or murdered her and then decided that they needed to clean and remove anything that might be evidence."

I started to mull this over. "Chief, this seems weird to me because if they cleaned up, maybe they took a shower in my parents' bathroom. If that was true, why wouldn't you have found their DNA in the shower or tub?"

"There was no DNA from people outside your family. We checked."

"Maybe they wore something to keep themselves clean, like one of those white coveralls. Then nobody would recognize them."

"You mean a hazmat suit?"

"I guess so. I've been having these strange dreams about the house, and in them a person came up the front walk in a hoodie, but it could have been a hazmat suit. One time we had a workman come to Grandma and Grandpa's house to work. He wore one. He called it a 'bunny suit.' If they wore that, I think maybe somebody might have seen them."

"You forget that the medical examiner pinpointed the time of the murder at 6:30 AM. In February it's still dark."

"But a white suit? You could see that, right?"

The Chief frowned. He was thinking. "The person might have worn a black- or dark-colored coverall. Then they couldn't be seen, or maybe they wore a white suit so they couldn't be seen in the snow."

I was thinking, too. "Maybe they wore a black coat over the white coveralls, black hat, black boots, mask. Gloves, so there'd be no fingerprints. They could sneak around in the dark and no one would see them. But what happened to all those clothes?"

"I think from a practical viewpoint, the person didn't wear a coat."

"That's right," I said. "OK, here's my theory: The murderer wore white, was watching the house waiting for my father to leave for work. After he left, they came in through the door that my father used, and maybe Dad forgot to lock it."

"That would explain some of it," he said. "Just remember, there were no witnesses. We interviewed everyone in the neighborhood, the workmen, the delivery guy, everyone! No results at all."

"So, it had to be someone who walked right in through the unlocked door."

"Or maybe," said the Chief, "the person had a key."

The server approached with hot water and more decaf. My hands were so cold. It felt good to hold the warm cup, but despite the warmth, the rest of me felt chilled. I was shivering a bit, those emotional shivers that I got whenever I felt some powerful feelings. Chief Langdon asked me if I wanted something to eat. I wasn't hungry, but hot food would be a distraction that might also help with the shivers.

I looked up at the server, "I think I'll have a burger and fries," I said.

"Make it two," the Chief added.

Out of the manila folder, Chief Langdon produced some photos of the house. The footprints, the entrance to the back door, the front door with footprints. But where did the footprints originate? I couldn't tell. The snow was all messed up and there was no sign of where the murderer came from. So, I asked him.

"For a few days before the murder, your parents were having some work done in the house. The furnace wasn't working properly and there was a repairman there. Plus, the man came to read the electric meter, UPS delivered a package, and the letter carrier was delivering the mail. There were hundreds of footprints in the snow. A few were from heavy boots like the murderer wore. We couldn't figure out where the footprints came from because of all the activity in the snow. Lots of walking from house to house. Lots of footprints."

"So maybe it was a workman who killed her," I said.

"We followed up on that, and we hit a dead end with our investigation."

"How did you separate the boot prints of the murderer from the boot prints of the workmen?" I asked.

"We had to weed out sizes and brands. We identified one pair that seemed to be unique, not like any of the other boots. Those prints may belong to the murderer."

Then I asked the chief, "Where do we look now? All we have are boot footprints and the ax for hard evidence. If the area in and around the house, the mud, the snow, wasn't leading to anything, maybe I need to look at the people around my mother more closely."

"You're getting the hang of this, Mari," he said with a smile. "Now you need to make a list of your suspects and why you suspect them."

"So that's what you have in the spare bedroom. If I put together a list and send it to you, can you compare it to what you have and let me know if we match?"

"That would be great. Maybe between the two of us we can figure this out."

"And one more question. What about me? I was there. Didn't I cry? Wasn't I hungry?

Your dad was already home. He was the one who called 911. We got there right away.

He had taken you out of your crib and changed your clothes. He told us that there was a bottle of milk in your crib with you. In the morning he used to leave a bottle for you before he left so your mother could sleep a little later. He said you'd find the bottle and after you drank it, you'd fall back to sleep. We wanted to test you to see if they had drugged you, but you were pretty upset, and he didn't want you to be even more upset by a needle. He had washed the bottle and refilled it with milk because you were so hungry from being alone all day."

I looked at Chief Langdon and felt tears coming. First, I felt sad for the little girl who was alone all day with a bottle of milk and her mother's body. Then I was touched that Chief was asking for my opinion, believing me, and wanting to see all the work I had done up to this point. Wow! That felt amazing! Suddenly my chills went away, and I was starving. The hamburger and fries arrived and tasted great. Maybe I'd even have warm apple pie for dessert with a scoop of vanilla ice cream melting on top.

The chief had more stuff in the folder he was carrying. "What else do you have?" I asked.

"Pictures of the body and the coroner's report." He showed me the report, but he closed the folder and said, "I can't show you the photos of your mother's body. I think they're just too horrible for you to see. Today has been a very tough day for you, hasn't it? Maybe we should call it a day."

Even though the food had made me feel better, everything that Chief Langdon and I had talked about got a lot of emotions stirred up. I was angry, sad, exhausted, relieved, and yes, even happy. I was happy to get all that missing information, happy that I had some information to offer that was being listened to, and happy that the chief was still searching for my mother's killer even after fifteen years. He handed me a brown envelope with copies of my mother's file.

"Mari, the from the crime scene are in there. You can look at them if you want when youget home, or maybe you don't want to look at them at all. Like I said, they're horrific."

"Thanks so much for meeting with me and sharing this information," I said. "I have some ideas about who might have committed the murder, but I'm not sure if I can share them just yet. I need to organize my thoughts and just maybe I'll look at the pictures."

I knew for sure I'd be looking at the pictures tonight.

"Let me know soon, Mari."

"Yes, I will. But I'd like to visit your house one more time. Do you think that could happen?"

"Sure. Maybe Brenda could put you up."

"I'm not sure I want Brenda involved," I said. "I have to figure out travel and a place to stay."

"Why don't you want her involved?" he asked. "Is she on your list of suspects?"

"She just makes me uncomfortable, that's all. She texts me a few times every day. I can't explain it, but that's another thing I need to think about."

"What does she text you about?"

"Nothing specific unless she's planning a trip here. Mostly I think she wants to be in touch with me and check to see where I am." He had a quizzical look on his face, like somehow it made little sense to him. It made little sense to me, too.

"How much longer will you be in Rochester?"

"I'll be leaving on Monday, around noon."

"OK, I'll text you with any updates."

I left the restaurant and ran into Emily's dad in the lobby.

"Hey kiddo. How did it go?" he asked.

"It was a lot of information and I'm a little tired. I think I'll take the bus home."

"I can take you now. There aren't any workshops for me this afternoon, so I left early. I was looking for you when you found me."

"That's great," I said. I was still a little distracted by what I had learned, but I tried to work up a smile. We went to the hotel garage and got in the car.

As he pulled onto the expressway, Mr. Reese asked, "Did Chief Langdon help you learn anything new?'

"Yeah, he did. But I need to think stuff over to see where it's going."

"OK, if you need any help, just let me know." He made that offer again.

"Maybe I'll ask you for some help later on." I said. "But not right now."

"Just so you know, the chief has a fantastic reputation in law enforcement, but what's more important is his reputation as an honest, caring person. You can trust him. I'm wondering if Chief Langdon might like to join us for dinner tomorrow night. I'll ask him when I see him at the conference tomorrow. Would you like to come?"

"You'd better believe it," I said. "You know what else, Mr. Reese? I need to go to Danbury to see our family's house again. Do you have any ideas about how I could get there?"

"Let me work on that and I'll get back to you." he said, with a smile.

Chapter 28

No one was home when I got there. I was totally energized, so I went upstairs to the attic to hunt through boxes again. There was a carton of stuffed animals and toys, including a doll that looked like me in a dress that looked like the one I was wearing in my one-year-old baby picture. Same clothes, same hair. Must have cost a lot. I wondered who bought it? I bet it was Grandma. I heard a car in the driveway and saw Grandma and Grandpa get out. Good. I could ask Grandma if she bought it for me. I started downstairs, but I stopped when I heard them talking in the kitchen, Grandma's voice first.

"I hate Mari going downtown to meet with that police chief," she said. "She's too obsessed with this murder. I wish she'd leave it alone. The police can handle it."

"Evidently not well enough," said Grandpa. "It's been over 15 years, Carol. They stopped looking a long time ago. It's a cold case. Winds up in a drawer. Mari is right. It needs to be brought up again. What's your objection?"

"I'm worried about her. She asked to go to the cemetery today to see Marianne's grave. She brought a flower and got emotional when she saw the grave. She wanted to know why we buried Marianne in a single plot."

"What did you tell her?"

"I told her that her father was in a hurry to get the burial over with. What else was I going to tell her?"

"That was probably the best answer, but it's still weak. She's a smart girl and won't accept an answer if it doesn't seem to fit. She's been that way since she was in preschool, remember?"

"I couldn't tell her how angry he was at Marianne. She doesn't need to know that. It raises too many questions and puts her father in a nasty spot."

What did they mean by that? I don't think I was ready to find out. I made some noise on the stairs so they'd hear me.

"Mari, is that you?" Grandma called.

"Yes, it is," I said as I walked down the stairs. "I found this doll in one box. Did you buy this for me? It looks just like me."

"Oh, my gosh, I forgot all about that doll. Sure, I did. It was a gift for your first birthday." She took the doll in her hands and straightened the ruffles on its dress.

"I bet it cost a lot of money," I said. "Matching the picture and my clothes couldn't have been easy."

"I don't remember," she said, "But whatever it cost, you were worth it. Still are." And she put her arm around me and leaned her head on mine. "So now, if you don't mind, I need to put the groceries away."

Chief Langdon accepted the dinner invitation from the Reeses. Mrs. Reese invited my entire family, too. I wanted to watch the interaction between my dad, my grandparents, and the chief. They all knew each other from the murder investigation, so I was sure there would be some uncomfortable and interesting dinner moments. Dad didn't come. He said he had a meeting at work. Maybe he did. Or maybe he didn't want to see the chief. Grandma and Grandpa were silent. I could see that they weren't very comfortable. The conversation was about the differences between the Rochester police and the Danbury police. The men talked a little about the conference. Grandpa joined in. In the middle of it all, I got a text from Brenda.

Mari, can you call me? Need to talk. It was the third text today, but it would need to wait until after dinner.

The chief was getting ready to go, but he pulled me aside. "Listen, Mari, if you find anything else out, call me. And when you come to Danbury, let me know."

"Thanks, Chief. I will. I'm working on getting there." We shook hands, and he gave me a nod that made me feel very reassured. I would solve this!

My grandparents went home, but I stayed to talk to Emily. We headed upstairs to her room.

"So, tell me what's going on." She said.

"Lots of stuff. Mostly Brenda is getting on my nerves."

"What's she doing?'

"At least once a day she texts me, sometimes more. Nothing specific, just asks how things are going."

"Maybe she's worried about you." Emily said, always the optimist.

"I don't think so. I think she wants to know what I've found out about the murder. There's something not right."

"Does she know that Chief Langdon was here?"

"I'm not sure," I said. "Unless he told her."

"Well, Jake is taking care of the dog, so I'm sure she knows that he was away."

"How is Jake?" I asked.

"He's good. Just waiting for college acceptance letters, like everybody else. He wants to come here over the Christmas break."

"I guess Brenda will be here, too. I wonder if that's what she was texting about. She wants me to call her."

"It's still early. Why don't you call her now?"

"Because I don't want her to believe that just because she called, I was anxious to get back to her."

"But you are. You want to know what she wants, right?"

"I do, but I want her to wait for my call. I'll call her back tomorrow. Please don't tell Jake about this, OK?"

"I think he already knows. He told me she's been trying to get in touch. He's trying to plan the Christmas trip here, but she wants to come too. She wants to make sure you'll be around."

"I wonder what she has in mind," I said, more to myself than to Emily.

Then, "Hey Emily, what if we go there? I want to go back to see Chief Langdon's house again. He said I could, but I just need to get to Danbury."

"That could work. We'd need to figure out transportation, though."

"Yup. We could leave the day after Christmas, stay for two or three days, and come back before New Year's Eve. That's a wonderful idea because I could spend New Year's Eve with Seth before he goes back to Boston. Let's think about it and come up with a plan."

Brenda was giving me the creeps. Her texting was getting out of hand, and I needed to discourage her because it was so creepy. For every three texts she sent, I'd return one. I kept them short, sending emojis when I could. Most of the texts were just to keep in touch. Brenda would write: *How are you doing?* Me: Smiley face emoji. Brenda: *How's school?* Me: Thumbs up emoji. *Have you finished cleaning out the attic?* Me: Sad face emoji. But the one I dreaded was, *when can we get together?* I felt so ambivalent about seeing her. She had been my mother's best friend, so there was that connection, but there was something weird about her being on me so much. I wondered if she had other friends. That was something I could ask Jake about. I typed, *Working on it!* and added a smiley face, but I wasn't really smiling.

Chapter 29

Em and I had not come up with a plan, and I needed to talk to Jake to find out if his father agreed to talk to me. That might factor into whatever Em and I worked out. I called him and asked if he had heard from his dad.

"I heard from him, Mari. He says he'll talk, but he wants to do it face-to-face. He's close to Rochester if you can believe that! He wouldn't be more specific about the town, but he has a small farm there and a herd of beef cattle, about twelve steers and a few cows for breeding. He said he'd find a place to meet and give us some dates.

"Doesn't sound like he lives on a bus line, but I can probably do it if you get the directions for me."

"He says he still doesn't want anyone to know where he is."

I promised Jake that I wouldn't tell anyone. He gave me his father's number, and that night I called him from my room. He answered on the second ring.

"Mr. Henderson? This is Mari Franklin."

"Hi Mari. I appreciate your keeping my location a secret. Jake told me you're trying to solve your mother's murder. What can I do to help?

"I wonder if we can get together and talk?" I asked.

"As long as you keep my location a secret, I'd be glad to do that."

"Where can we meet? You probably don't want to come here," I said. "Too risky."

"Correct. But maybe we could meet at a church near here. I do some handyman work for them, and I can ask the pastor if we can use an office there to meet. The church is in Geneva. Do you know how to get to Geneva?"

"I sure do. My friends and I went there to look at the college. There's also a bus that goes there. That'll work."

He gave me the church address, and we set the meeting for next Saturday.

I was glad we were meeting at the church. There probably would be people around, and I was feeling safer about meeting with him. Even though he said he had nothing to do with the murder, I was still nervous about meeting him alone, and because I swore not to tell anyone about him, I couldn't take one of my friends with me. It also meant I needed to take the bus and make up a story about why I was going to Geneva when I would rather drive there.

I made a list of questions I wanted to ask him, but I realized that Chief Langdon should be my first stop. I needed more background information because I was feeling a little too iffy about everything. I postponed the meeting, and I called him back and told him I'd get back to him about it.

"That's okay," he said. "Whenever you're ready, I'll still be here."

Chapter 30

It was about ten o'clock when I heard my dad come home. As he came upstairs and passed by my room, I opened the door.

"Hi, Dad," I said. "Can we talk for a minute?" I wanted to ask him about Mom's grave.

"Sure. What's up?"

"I wondered why Mom is buried in that boring cemetery and why is she buried in a plot by herself?"

"Mari, you ask the toughest questions sometimes. Can I sit down?"

I invited him into the room, and he sat in the desk chair, which he turned around to face me as I sat on the bed.

"The night before your mother was killed, we had an argument. She wanted to leave Danbury and move to this area. My job wasn't going well, so I wasn't happy either. You know how it is. Sometimes you argue and it carries over depending on how big the argument was. When I found her body, the anger welled up at everyone. At whoever did it, but also at her."

"Why her?"

"We never finished the argument, and then she died. I was left with our lives in a mess, and you and I had to go back to Rochester. Your mother won the argument after all. Our family didn't have a burial plot, so the funeral director suggested the cemetery and I must admit that I wasn't thinking of anything else but getting this horrible thing behind us, so I left it up to him. When he asked if we wanted a family plot, I told him that was not on my mind. A single grave would be fine."

"But Dad, she was the victim here."

"I know. I probably was in shock, too. Not making good decisions. I hope that I answered your question. I would give anything to take back that anger and the last words we spoke, which were probably not nice. I would give anything to have your mother alive and with us today."

"Me too. Maybe we can talk about moving her to the other cemetery with a family plot and a beautiful headstone."

Dad smiled and said, "We'll talk about that another time. Maybe Spring. The ground will be frozen until then."

He was right. I hadn't thought about that. He left to go to his room.

I thought this might be a good time to look at the pictures of the murder scene that Chief Langdon gave me. I took out the folder and opened it. There was my mother lying in her bed. Her face and head were bloody. There was so much blood it was hard to tell her hair color. The ax was next to her head, the blade covered with blood. It was so horrible I thought I might throw up. I wanted to look at the pictures, but at the same time, I wanted to look away. What a terrible scene. I began to cry and I hoped that my mother didn't know what was happening. I put the pictures back in the folder and stuck them in a drawer in my desk so I couldn't see them. I went to bed unsure if I would get any sleep.

Chapter 31

I was missing Seth and wouldn't be seeing him again until Christmas break. We'd known each other for so long that when he left for college, it only added to the feelings of loss I always had for my mother. Losses in my life always seemed to go back to missing her. I could lose my math book tomorrow and it could set me off into remembering that my mother was gone. So, with Seth, it was even harder because he was first, an excellent friend, but second, I had feelings for him. We were becoming a couple, which was so great but so sad when we were apart. At least we had texts and Facetime. But even then, I still missed him.

Seth and I were friends even when we were little. A group of us, me, Seth and Emily and a few other kids used to play in the woods behind my house. We built forts and planned to build real log cabins, one for each of us. I remember one time we set up rocks for a foundation and hunted for wood for the walls. I bet the unfinished cabin is still there. One time when we were out on one of our hiking adventures, I fell and broke my arm. I couldn't pull myself up because my arm hurt so much! Seth helped me up and walked me back to my house. He was a Boy Scout and had taken First Aid, so he knew what to do. He made a sling out of his shirt and gently fixed my arm into it, which helped with the pain. I think I fell in love with him that day, even though I was twelve and he was thirteen.

Whenever he was away, I could concentrate on the pictures of him on my phone. Seth was smart, but not in a show-off way. If a problem came up, it was not unusual to see him standing or sitting off to the side with a look of concentration on his face. I love that look... when he's lost in thought. He listened and he watched everything and everyone in the room. His eyes focused on the thing he was thinking about, and he was right in there, right with that thought until he reached solution or a conclusion. Seth and I talked about my mother's murder from time to time, but since he went off to college, there was not enough time to talk about the things I found out. He was interested in helping me solve this. But it was still very important to me that I find the murderer on my own. I saw it as a way of showing my commitment to my mother.

Without Seth around, I contacted the next-best person I knew, Emily. Then I called Nicole and Jodi and invited them over to help me finish up the stuff in the attic. Jodi and Nicole hadn't been up there yet, but they seemed excited to dig through some old boxes. I made some brownies, which made the house smell great. After everyone arrived, I brought a plate of brownies up to the attic and we each grabbed a glass of cold milk to go with them.

"What's here for us to do?" Jodi asked.

The last time I worked on this project, I grouped the boxes, and we had only six left. Then I told my friends about the three different handwriting on the sides of the boxes: those of my dad, my grandmother, and my mother. Whoever had packed the box probably labeled it. The ones packed by my mother were the oldest and might tell me something about her and about our lives together before she died, or about my parents' lives before I was born. She would have packed stuff important to her, things she wanted to save for a reason. Like with the baby clothes, maybe she was planning to have another baby. Or she could have saved them to show them to me when I got older. I thought we'd be less likely to find anything meaningful in the stuff packed by Dad or Grandma, but I never knew. I decided that we should start with the stuff Grandma packed to get that out of the way.

Jodi said, "How come you're picking the stuff your grandma packed to go next?"

"I don't know. Maybe I picture my grandmother choosing more emotional, more connected stuff than my father, who'd most likely choose more practical things like tools." I pointed to a box with my grandmother's printing on the side and asked Jodi to go through it.

She pulled off the tape and looked inside. The box was full of tablecloths and napkins, all monogrammed with a fancy "F." Somehow, I couldn't imagine my parents using this stuff. Jodi said. "This is nice. Maybe your grandmother forgot about it. She might want to use it for the holidays. You should ask her." I asked Jodi to go through all the stuff and put sets together, tablecloths and napkins that matched. I gave her some pins so she could group the napkins together with their matching tablecloth. She organized six sets, and we put them aside to show Grandma.

Nicole went ahead without me. She found a box full of towels. Like the table linens, there seemed to be sets also, all with a big "F" monogram. Nicole organized them and found three sets of towels, except that one of the big blue bath towels was missing. There were six hand towels and six facecloths, but only five bath towels.

"Huh. What do you think happened to the other towel?" Nicole asked. I wondered what had happened to the bath towel, too. Was it the same towel that my parents used and left in the bathroom the day they killed my mother? Was there a logical reason for its disappearance, or had someone taken it? Just the same, we put the ones we found with the table linens to bring downstairs.

Em found another box. My father had labeled this one. "This one is heavy." She said to me as she opened it. "Whoa," she said. "Look at this."

I looked inside to see a bunch of tools and a metal toolbox. We opened the toolbox and found some hammers, some screwdrivers, a wrench, the usual stuff. Also in the box was a small ax, maybe more of a hatchet. I knew it wasn't the murder weapon because Chief Langdon said that ax was with the evidence from the murder. But it was enough to make me catch my breath.

Em put her arm around my shoulder, and Jodi and Nicole came over, looked in the box and looked at each other. Jodi took my hand and Nicole covered the box.

"What should we do with this box?" Jodi asked. "Maybe we should just toss it or bring it to Goodwill. They can get rid of it. You don't need it around to remind you."

"The tools aren't the only things that remind me. Having them around or getting rid of them won't make a difference. I'm reminded every day, especially now when I'm so focused on finding the murderer. Listen, all of you. You're my best friends. I'll never forget how much we've shared, especially our awesome road trip to look at colleges, how you helped me get to Danbury and how you're helping me now. You're helping with the boxes, but you're helping me by standing next to me during this entire thing."

Then I cried, then Nicole started, and then Emily and Jodi started crying, too. We were standing in a circle, and we linked arms and had a group hug, all of us crying and hanging on to each other. After a few minutes, Jodi said, "Enough of this. We've got to get back to work."

I could always count on Jodi to pull us back into reality.

Only three more boxes. One was labeled in my mother's writing, "Christmas," and was full of ornaments. We all looked through them. They looked brand new, but some glass ones had lost some of their color after all this time. But there was one with a bride and groom on it, "Our First Christmas" it said. Another had a pink angel on it, "Baby's First Christmas," and it had my name engraved under the angel's feet. The rest of the ornaments didn't look very special, so I took out the two that meant a lot to me, and we put the box aside.

Nicole opened the next box that had Grandma's writing on the side. Labeled, "throws," and was full of crocheted blankets, the type I put over myself when I curled up on the couch to watch TV. There were four blankets, all in various colors and patterns. But the one at the bottom of the box was pink, blue and green. The colors matched the wallpaper in my bedroom at 43 Windthorne Road. I wondered if my mother put it over us when she held me in the rocking chair. It was pretty and so sweet that Grandma packed it. I took the blanket and put it in an empty box with my doll, the teething ring, the album of baby pictures, my baby book, the Christmas ornaments, and my mother's calendar.

Finally, we got to the last box. Nicole brought it to me and put it in my lap. It had my mother's writing on the side and while it wasn't very heavy; it wasn't light either. I opened it up slowly and looked inside. Books. Fifteen books. In each book were two pages in my mother's handwriting. I took out one page that had the title of the book, the author's name, and a list of women's names at the top. There were no names I recognized.

"They look like meeting minutes," Emily said. "That's how we record our Science Club minutes at school."

"Maybe it's a book club," I said. "My mother loved to read, and Brenda brought me a box of books she had borrowed from my mother and forgot to return. Maybe these are more of the same books."

"Do the other books have notes in them, too?" Nicole asked.

"I don't think so. But I can check." I ran down the attic stairs to my bedroom and knelt to look under the bed where I had put the box that Brenda brought me. I pulled it out and opened it. I picked up each book and ruffled through the pages. There were no papers. I walked back up the stairs to the attic where my friends were waiting.

"Nothing," I said.

"Do you think maybe Brenda took the notes out?"

"Why would she do that?"

Just then, my phone beeped with a text. It was Brenda. I turned to my friends and asked, "How does she know when I'm talking about her?"

"Maybe she's a witch," Jodi said. She made a scary face and curled her fingers so her hands hooked like claws.

Everything OK? she wrote.

I texted her back. *Still cleaning out the attic and going through boxes. Also went through the box of books you brought. Did you throw away any papers that were in those books?*

Then came a beep. *No. Those were books we read, and she and I talked about them when we walked with you and Jake in the mornings, kind of like our own private book club. Are you coming to Danbury soon?*

I texted back, *Not sure. Will let you know.*

My friends and I took the box with all my baby stuff, the blanket, my mother's calendar, Christmas ornaments, album and the doll that was my twin and the box with Mom's book club books and the box full of linens along with the plate of brownies and milk and went downstairs to my room.

"What are you going to do with this stuff?" Em said, looking a little exasperated.

I understood her feelings. My friends had been so involved in my goal of solving my mother's murder right now that I was feeling guilty for involving them. They were wearing out. I needed to take over this quest completely and rely more on Chief Langdon. My friends didn't need this anymore.

"Well," I sighed, "I'll keep the sentimental stuff for myself. The books might be valuable for Chief Langdon to look at. I really need to get back to Danbury to show this stuff to him."

Nobody suggested another road trip, which backed up my theory that I had burned them out on this. Normally they'd be up to drive there. I think the upcoming Christmas holidays were an enormous factor, too.

"Listen, you three are my best friends. You've been the best during this. I need to do this for myself and my mother. I need you to be around for me and I'll ask you when I need help, like I did today. But I'll be going at this on my own."

"OK," Em said, "But if you need us, you need to let us know, because we'll be here for you–at least if you make brownies for us."

We all laughed, and I promised to make more brownies for them, and I told them I might even add chocolate frosting.

"Then we'll definitely be there for you!" Jodi stood up and put her hands on her hips like a superhero.

Chapter 32

Once again, how was I going to get to Danbury? I texted Chief Langdon to work out some dates. I needed to have time off from school, and I had family holiday stuff, although aside from Christmas and New Year's, we didn't have much scheduled. Grandma and Grandpa always planned to visit the homeless shelter to give out gifts and food baskets to needy families the week before Christmas. When I was little, I went with them and brought little stuffed animals for the kids. Anyway, I talked with Grandma about my plans. She sat and listened and said, "Mari, let's get your father in here and run this past him." We all went into the family room to sit. Dad threw some logs on the fire.

He turned back to Grandma and said, "Looks like you chopped enough wood for the whole winter, Mom."

"I wish!" she said. "Tell your dad what you're planning, Mari."

I told Dad about my plans to go to Danbury to see Chief Langdon's house again. The chief was open to several dates, but I needed transportation.

Dad said, "It's very complicated to get there by train and bus. You really need to drive. I wish you wouldn't go. But given the time of year and the weather, it's kind of risky to go by yourself, or at least that's the way I feel about it."

"Why do you need to go there again?" Grandma asked.

I explained to them how I found several important things in the attic, stuff that was purely sentimental, yet some that could point to clues leading to the murderer.

"What clues?" asked Dad.

"Oh, just books and papers. I need to go through everything. I just skimmed through stuff when I was cleaning out, and when my friends were with me, I didn't have time to look carefully. But I found some of your tools, Dad, and nice linens, Grandma. Maybe these are things you could use. Somebody must have packed them back in Danbury."

Grandma wrinkled her nose like she did when she was thinking. "I'm sure I packed a lot of it. Maybe Grandpa packed the tools."

"There were several sets of towels. One set, the blue one, was missing a big towel, but the blue towels were monogrammed. I bet the missing bath towel was monogrammed, too, with a big, navy blue 'F.'"

Grandma's nose wrinkled again. "I think those were all wedding presents or gifts for your mother's bridal shower. People liked to give things with monograms in those days."

"Do you remember what happened to the missing towel?" I asked.

"Boy, I can't remember at all. Could be we just left it behind, or maybe it was in the wash."

Grandma looked at Dad and said, "Maybe it's time to go upstairs and make some decisions about what's up there."

"Let's go," I said. And the three of us went up to the attic. I told them I had taken a box downstairs to look at, mostly books but also the other interesting things. Grandpa, who had been on an errand, returned to find us all in the attic and joined us. He recognized the tools.

"Oh boy, I remember packing those." he said. "Most of them were new. We went to the hardware store to buy them, right, Ed? I think we even bought the big ax that day, didn't we?"

Dad looked down at his shoes, then quietly said, "I remember."

That had to be a rough memory. Being up here, around my mother's stuff, was very emotional for me. But I couldn't even imagine how emotional it was for my dad and grandparents. They were at 43 Windthorne. They saw the body. They had to deal with the horror, the reality of the murder of someone they loved. Well, at least I knew my dad loved her. Grandma and Grandpa seemed attached to her, but maybe only because of Dad and me. I guessed I'd never be able to understand that whole relationship.

Later, I went to my room to do my homework. Grandpa came to my room. This was very unlike Grandpa. Grandma did most of the talking and acting. Grandpa hung out in the background, so it surprised me to see him at my door.

"May I come in?"

"Of course," I couldn't help but wonder what he wanted.

"How are you doing with all of this?" he asked with a lot of concern.

"I'm doing OK, just trying to go through my mother's stuff to look for clues and planning my next move. Do you have any clues for me? Any ideas about who did this?"

"Yes, I do, but anything I would come up with would be guesswork. I think you need to work with the police chief–what was his name again?"

"Chief Langdon."

"Yes. Well, I want you to be safe. I worry that if you got too close to the murderer, you might be at risk. As strange as the chief is, what with buying that house and all, and living there too, I know he'd be sure you were safe."

That was true. I believed that Chief Langdon would watch out for me, too.

"I really want to work with him, but he's in Danbury and I'm here."

Grandpa took my hand and said, "You know, sweetheart, I really cared about your mother. I thought she and your dad were great together. Her death was a tremendous loss to this small family, especially to you. That the murder was never solved makes me furious, too. I will do everything I can to help you. What do you need?"

"I need some way to get to Danbury."

I couldn't believe what he was saying about my mother. I never knew how strong his feelings were about her. And getting this offer of help was amazing! But I wanted to ask him some other things about his feelings.

How did you feel when she and Dad got married? She was already expecting me, so was that a problem for you?"

"Not really. Like I said, I really liked her. Her smile could light up the room. She was bright and friendly, and she really loved your dad. My only objection was that they were young, but lots of people get married young. They were pretty determined to make it work, so I backed them."

"What do you mean, you 'backed them?'"

"Grandma wasn't too happy. She thought they were too young. Sometimes she and your mother would get into a battle of wills over some things."

"Like what?"

"Oh, where you three would live, for example. She wanted you all to stay in Rochester since she wanted to be a grandmother to you."

"But Grandpa, didn't they go to Danbury because Dad got a job there?"

"Yes, that's true. But your mother was really pushing to leave. I wonder if she thought Grandma would try to be too involved in your lives. It was a battle between two strong women, I can tell you that much. I see that same glint in your eye when you get an idea to do something."

"What glint is that?"

"The glint of determination. You've become a strong woman like your mother, Mari. You look like her, but you think a lot like her too, and your eyes light up in the same way. And I can't help but wonder if living all these years with your grandmother hasn't incorporated some of Grandma's determination, too." His face lit up with a big smile, "This murderer does not understand who he's dealing with!"

"'He' Grandpa? Do you think it's a man?"

"I didn't say that. As they say on the crime tv shows, 'Follow the clues.'"

"I intend to. But like I said, I need to get to Danbury with them."

"Tell you what, I'll lend you my car so you can get there. When are you planning to leave?"

"Really, Grandpa? OMG I never thought you would do that for me!"

"It was that glint of determination that did it," he said. "Your mother's spirit, I guess."

I put my hand on my locket and felt its warmth. "Grandpa, thanks so much!" I gave him a hug and an enormous smile. As I snuggled into his shoulder, I could smell the fabric softener in his soft flannel shirt. "I hope to go over Christmas break. I'll let you know what days soon."

Chapter 33

I was still getting two or three texts a day from Brenda asking me when I was coming. Now that I had the car, all I needed was a date and a place to stay. Although I was sure she'd want me, I didn't feel comfortable staying at her place for a couple of reasons. First, I was afraid I'd let something slip about her husband and the fact that I knew where he was. If I stayed with her, and Jake was there–why wouldn't he be? It was Christmas break–it would be hard for us to talk about his dad without his mother hearing us, or at least becoming suspicious. And one more thing. She was starting to scare me a little. I still didn't like all this compulsive texting. I called Jake on our secret phone to ask him for suggestions, and he started off by suggesting I stay with them. He got very persuasive, but the more he pressed me to consider their house, the more and more I felt uncomfortable. I asked him pointedly about what his dad might think about it.

"I guess you're right," he answered. "It would be too risky for him." That got me off the hook for sure.

"So, what day?"

"I'll aim for the 18th, but I need to talk to the chief first, and I also need to make a hotel reservation."

"All right, just let me know what you set up."

"Fine. Let your mother know so she stops texting me."

"Let her know yourself. I don't want her wondering why we were in touch and give away info about my dad."

"Ok," I said. I hung up, then I called Chief Langdon. "I'm planning to come to Danbury the week before Christmas," I told him.

"Do you know where you're staying?" he asked.

"I'll try to get a hotel room, but it may be tough because of the holiday. I'll let you know the arrangements."

"OK, Mari, I'm not going anywhere. It's quiet around here during the holidays, just me and the dog. You're the first company I've had around Christmas and I'm looking forward to seeing you."

"Me too, Chief. I'll be in touch."

Here was this guy and his dog, alone in a murder house for all these years. His entire life –well, at least for the past fifteen years– has been my mother's murder and finding who did it. Then again, that sounded a lot like me. Was I going to be living my life that way? I sure hope not. I wanted a solution to this terrible crime so I could move on with college and the rest of my life. Although if I didn't solve it, I'd at least like a dog to keep me company too. Maybe I should do a little Christmas shopping and bring gifts for him and the dog. I was getting attached to them both.

I texted Chief Langdon. *I have Grandpa's car. Let's pick a date. I get off from school the week before–actually December 18. I could leave early on the 19th and be at your place by lunchtime.*

He sent me a thumbs up.

Things were getting real.

Chapter 34

The nineteenth took forever to arrive. The decorations were up, and we trimmed the tree. I made some cookies for Chief Langdon and bought a toy and chew bone for his dog. A warm coat, gloves and a full tank of gas and I was ready to go. I brought the things we had rescued from the attic–the doll, the picture albums, the baby book, the boxes of books that were my mother's and her desk calendar. I hugged Grandpa and Grandma goodbye. Grandma wasn't too happy about my trip, but she packed me a lunch. Grandpa gave me the car keys, a hug and a smile, and slipped a gas credit card into my hand. He whispered in my ear, "Go get 'em, Mari."

I smiled back at him, "Thanks Grandpa, for everything." Dad told me to be careful and gave me a kiss, and then I headed for the Thruway.

It was one of those rare days in Upstate New York when the sun was shining. I drove the same route that I had taken with my friends and as I drove, I thought about that trip. I started laughing as I thought about the teasing and the joking we did. They were exceptional friends to rearrange their lives to go with me on that original trip. I thought too about what we talked about in the car; how we all shared the scariest moments in our lives, and believe me, they were scary.

I'm sure Nicole was frightened of moving and going to a new school. I've seen new kids being watched for any sign of being different, if their clothes were different, if their hair was different, if their speech was different. I'm sure that this existed in Nicole's old school, and kids who were different stood an excellent chance of being bullied. She came into our school scared; she probably knew what she was up against, but she was friendly and strong and luckily, she ran into us quickly. We reached out to her and wound up welcoming her into our group of friends.

Jodi was so afraid when people stopped her family when they were speaking Spanish. The fear she had of her family members being deported had to be intense. I heard a story about a man who was so frightened even though he was a citizen that he carried his passport with him all the time. I'm sure that threat doesn't go away.

And Emily, poor Emily, being afraid of being molested by a family friend. Tough. Standing up to him had to be scary, but she took care of herself. She locked all the doors. She told him he couldn't visit, and she called her father. Her father was such a good guy, but I could see what was scary for Emily. What if her father hadn't believed her? What if he'd believed her but did nothing about it? From what I know about Em's dad, neither seemed probable, but I was sure that was part of what was so scary to Emily. If Uncle Pete realized that no one would stop him, would he continue to get near her? She would not be a victim. I was sad that she never told me about it before. I would have backed her up too. I know it.

My friends had been through a lot that has made them strong; strong enough to stand behind me while I looked for my mother's murderer. I was so glad I had them. As I drove, I thought about what really scared me. The thought of my mother's murder was scary, and scariest of all was knowing that the murderer left me there all day with my mother's body. I wasn't a target, but I could have been. I went back over what I had done so far to find her murderer. I convinced my family that I needed to do this, convinced them to support me when for all this time it seemed as if no one was interested in finding her murderer: I went to Danbury, met Brenda and Jake, went to the house at 43 Windthorne Road, met Chief Langdon and visited my old home, the house where my mother was murdered. When I got back, I cleaned out the attic to look for clues, I met with the chief again, and now I was on my way to look for more clues and share what I'd learned with the police chief who had been working on this for fifteen years. That was scary, but I was doing it. We were a brave bunch of women, my friends and me. I smiled to think about that, to recognize how strong we all were. I also smiled at how I used the word, "women" when it seemed like only last summer, we were just four "girls." I was bragging a little, but so what? I was alone in the car, and nobody could hear what I was thinking.

Chapter 35

I only stopped once to eat the lunch Grandma packed and get a cup of coffee, so I arrived in Danbury a little after 1:00. I texted Jake to tell him I was in town, and I would set up a meeting with Chief Langdon. Then I called the chief and told him I was coming over.

"Great, Mari! I'll see you in a few minutes."

Chief Langdon and Buddy were waiting for me. Buddy recognized me and wagged his tail and gave me his paw. I unloaded the boxes full of stuff from the attic. The chief and I carried them into the house and upstairs to the hall outside the bedrooms. Taking out a set of keys, he unlocked the deadbolt on the door and the secondary lock on the doorknob and opened it. The dog went inside and over to a green pet bed in the corner and climbed in.

"Buddy likes to stay with me while I'm working, but he gets bored and likes to nap. I want him to be comfortable," said the chief.

At that point, I took my attention away from the dog and looked around the room. On one wall sat a desk made from an old door held up by two small filing cabinets. On top of the desk sat two desktop computers and a tablet. In the far-right corner was one of those "in and out" trays with papers in a small stack in each tray. In the left corner was a rack to hold manila folders that had four or five of them in distinct colors standing at attention. On the wall behind the desk was a huge whiteboard. My eyes were drawn to it when I saw–taped to it–a bunch of pictures, some news articles and phone messages on post-it notes. Writing in black and red marker was scattered throughout, and off to the side was a list of names.

The pictures were individual shots of my mother, father, me when I was three years old, my grandparents and Brenda and her husband. Then at the end of the board was a section covered with brown wrapping paper.

"What's under the paper?" I asked.

"Those pictures of the murder scene. I covered them so you didn't have to see them. I told you they're tough to take."

I had a copy in the file he had given me, but I hadn't been able to look at them. I was afraid of what I would see. I was glad he had them covered up.

"You're the only person I've ever let into this room. Not even Jake has been in here."

"Why not?" I asked. "I thought you guys were friends."

"I guess so, but it really doesn't concern him. This is my work, and I've devoted a lot of time to finding the killer. If I share clues or conclusions with just anyone, I could ruin the case. I'd rather keep everything confidential for now. Can you understand why I do it this way?" Would he be able to share anything with her without jeopardizing the case? Or, because it was her family, is this allowed? Or, because it's a cold case, the rules are different?

"Sure," I said, "And I won't tell anyone what you have here or what you're looking at."

"Thanks, Mari. I'm glad you're here and we can look at this together," he said.

Then I asked, "Why are you letting me in on what you found?"

"Because you have missing pieces of your mother's life and information about the people around her that I don't have. You're really committed to finding this killer, much more so than anyone else, so I know you're serious. Plus, you're very smart and have good instincts. We can help each other solve this."

We slid my boxes into the room and Chief Langdon closed the door, locked the deadbolt and the doorknob lock, and he and Buddy led the way downstairs.

So, there I was in Danbury, the secret keeper not only for Jake and his father but also for Chief Langdon. Both would be a challenge.

I went back to the hotel and dropped off my suitcase. I wanted to call home and tell everyone I got here safely, and then I wanted to call Emily and hear her voice. Emily picked it up after one ring. "What are you doing, Em?"

"Just wrapping Christmas presents, then I'll walk the dog. Everything OK? Have you seen Jake?"

"Everything is wonderful. I haven't seen Jake yet, but I'll see him a little later. I already got to bring all the stuff we found to the chief's house and up to his workroom."

"What was the room like?"

"It looked like an office, very organized and neat, and not a speck of dust. His dog remembered me, which was great. He's so friendly." I started talking about the dog, figuring that it would distract Emily from asking questions and would keep me from talking about the room.

"Do you have any messages for Jake?"

"No, we'll talk at our usual time. How was the drive?"

"Long. I'm pretty tired."

"Well, be careful. I'm thinking about you."

We hung up. Then I got a text from Brenda. *I heard you are here. Come for dinner tonight. We'll eat around 6:30.*

I texted her back. *See you then.*

Jake would be there, which was good. We could keep the conversation light if I worked hard at it. Then I could look around their house a little and look at 43 Windthorne Road from their windows to get a different view of where the murder took place. Too bad it would be dark by then. I might have been able to get some pictures.

I went to the hotel and curled up on the bed with my journal.

Time to write to Mom again. Keeping the journal was helpful because I could work on my thoughts and the progress I was making. I could also let my imagination go, to imagine me and my mother together and what my life would have been like if she'd lived. I'd always wanted it to be an ideal relationship, but I'm sure we'd argue occasionally like teenagers and their mothers did. Some girls at school really didn't get along with their mothers. Would my mom and I have been like that? I couldn't let my mind go there. No, we could've gotten along just fine. I liked to think we'd have been close, so that was how I wrote to her.

Dear Mom,

Here I am back in Danbury again. Tonight, I'm going to Brenda and Jake's house for dinner and to do some more snooping. Then tomorrow I will spend a lot of time with Chief Langdon at our house and see if together we can find some clues. I think we're getting closer, but I need you to help me, maybe aim me in the right direction. I wear your locket every day just to remind me of you. Not that I need reminding, but it's yours and I know you wanted me to wear it.

After I leave here and go back to Rochester, I'll be meeting with Jake's dad. I hope he can help, too. We'll all work together to solve this, Mom, and find who did this to you. I hope everything comes together soon. *Love, Mari.*

I arrived at Brenda and Jake's house just before 6:30, and Jake let me in, asking, "How was the drive?"

"Long and kind of boring," I said. "But I'm glad I'm finally here. Em is good, and she sends her love."

Brenda was in the kitchen making dinner, but she came out to say hello and gave me a hug. "Dinner will be ready soon."

"Great," I thought. "Time to visit alone with Jake."

"So, Jake, any chance I can go upstairs and look out the windows so I can check out what my house looks like from your second floor?"

He walked me toward the staircase. "Sure. Let's go."

The second floor resembled 43 Windthorne, "my house," the house next door, only it was a little smaller. At the top of the stairs was Jake's room. Jake walked to the desk and turned on the green banker's lamp overlooking a closed laptop and a small stack of textbooks. It was a simple room, with a double bed covered in a green-striped quilt, and light green curtains. Besides the desk chair, Jake had a comfortable-looking armchair, maybe for reading or talking on the phone. On the wall opposite the door was a big old dresser with a mirror hanging over it. A bookcase stood in the corner opposite the bed. I scanned the titles. Mostly history and biographies. Everything was in order and immaculate. It was unusual, I thought, for a college-aged boy to be so neat, with no posters, no bulletin boards, no pictures. Was I operating on a stereotype about men being messy? Maybe so.

I moved over to the window to see if I could see next door. No luck–wrong side of the house. We went across the hall and there was the bathroom. "I think I want to stop in here and wash my hands," I said, and I slipped into the bathroom and closed the door.

It was dark outside, but Brenda had a light illuminating the back yard. The chief also had none in his yard, so I could see from Brenda's to the back door of the chief's house. I tried to take a picture, but it was too dark out. There was snow on the ground and footprints from Brenda's back door across to the chief's place and back again. Must've been Jake's trail from when he went to take care of the dog or help with stuff. I washed and dried my hands and opened the door. "OK, what's next?"

"Well, my mother's room is over here next to the bathroom." He switched on the light. The room was neat and in order. A queen-sized bed, a dresser, a night table on each side of the bed, a book on one of them. I couldn't see the title, but I think it was a Sue Grafton mystery. The bed had a blue quilt, and blue and white drapes framed the windows. There was also an old-fashioned vanity with drawers on each side for makeup and stuff. On top of it was a hairbrush and a box of tissues. Nothing unusual here. The windows looked toward the chief's house, just like the bathroom window did. Again, I tried to get a picture, but no luck.

Jake motioned to the room next door to his. "This is the guest room."

It faced the front of the house, and as he switched on the light, I saw they used it as an office. There was a couch that looked like it pulled out into a bed, a desk, a computer, and a small file cabinet. Again, everything in order. This was the most orderly family I had ever seen. I wondered if Em knew this. Although she wasn't a total slob, she liked her surroundings a little more "relaxed." At least that's the way I described her. I wondered if the place always looked like this, neat as a pin, as Grandma would say. Or had they put everything in "apple pie order" (another of Grandma's sayings) before I arrived? Something didn't seem right, or maybe it was that we didn't keep our house in such order, so to me it seemed strange, almost cold. And as I looked out into the front yard, I noticed the curtains moving in the front window of the house across the street. Mr. Nosey was at it again.

While Jake and I were upstairs, I asked him about his father. "Have you heard from your dad?"

"Yes, I did. He told me you're waiting to meet with him until after you met with the chief again."

"I'll get in touch with him as soon as I get back. But I need to ask you a question. What do you think happened between your parents that caused your father to leave?"

Just then, Brenda called up the stairs. "Hey kids, come on down, dinner's ready!"

We walked down to the dining room. "Wow," I said. "It smells great. Is it chicken?"

"It sure is. It's Jake's favorite. Baked chicken and rice."

Dinner conversation was light. Brenda asked if I had seen Chief Langdon at all, and I told her I had dropped off some stuff from our attic for him to look at.

"What kind of stuff?"

"Just stuff," I said.

Her face registered a flicker of annoyance, but she controlled it and returned to her plate of chicken. Jake looked at me, then at his mother, then back at me as if he was expecting me to elaborate on what I had brought. I had already decided not to. What I was doing was only my business.

"This chicken is great," I said, to change the subject. "I can see why you like it."

"How long are you staying, Mari? You must be planning to get back before Christmas."

"I am, but I'm staying as long as the chief needs me to look through stuff with him. I can stay as long as the 24th and still make it home."

"What kind of stuff?" she asked again.

Jake seemed to squirm a little in his chair, knowing that I was trying to avoid any discussion about what the chief and I were doing.

"Some stuff from the attic, that's all."

"I heard he has an extensive file about the murder," she said. "All kinds of clues."

"Well, apparently not enough because he hasn't solved my mother's murder yet."

Brenda got that annoyed look on her face again and stood up. I think she realized I was stonewalling her, and she was done trying to get information.

"Well, you two, I will clean up the kitchen and go straight to bed. Mari, you're welcome to stay and talk."

"Do you need help with the cleanup?"

"No thanks, I have it under control."

"I'll leave in a few minutes," I said. "I'm tired from all that driving, so I'm going back to the hotel to get some sleep. The chief and I have an early day tomorrow."

There it was again, her look of annoyance. Only a flicker, but enough to tell me she was not happy with me. I put on my coat and boots and Jake walked me to the car.

"Maybe I can catch up with you tomorrow," he said. "I'll be around after I get home from work."

"Sounds good," I said, and got in the car. I got back to the hotel in about 10 minutes, went to my room and put on my pajamas. Then I called home to check in. Everything was good there. And then I called Emily.

"Hey Em, I've got a question. Have you ever been up to Jake's room?"

"Sure, twice."

"Did it strike you as strange? I mean, here is this high school senior and his room is just too neat."

"I don't know, I guess. I thought maybe he cleaned because I was coming."

"Em, it seems a bit too sterile. His mother's room is the same way.

"So, what are you thinking? That maybe they're zombies?"

"No. Be serious. If they were zombies, there'd be body parts all over the floor."

And we both laughed hysterically.

Chapter 36

At nine o'clock the next morning, I arrived at Chief Langdon's house and he and Buddy were waiting for me. He smiled, "Hi Mari. Ready to work?" Buddy wagged his tail. The three of us went upstairs to the office and Buddy curled up in his bed in the corner. Chief and I sat down. He had separated the stuff I brought into piles.

"Looks like you started without me," I said.

"Well, sort of. I organized what you brought into two categories, relevant and not relevant. The first thing I want you to do is to look at what I saw as not relevant and tell me why you brought it along. Convince me it's relevant. For example, tell me why you brought your baby book, *Baby's First Year*. Why did you think it was important?"

"I don't know. Maybe it was seeing so much of her handwriting. It was so personal and full of emotion for me. Maybe I thought there would be a secret hint in there, a message about her life."

"All I see is a very happy young woman, proud of her new baby and everything you did. But what it tells me is that accuracy was important to her. She was into recording things. Your weight, your height, how many times you rolled over and in which direction, how many visits she made with you to the pediatrician. She was very exact. You might be right. This could be a clue, but more a clue about her personality than a direct clue hidden in what she had written. Her writing spanned almost two years before they murdered her. Not only that, but she also put it away in the box with your baby clothes. At that point I wouldn't think she was hiding clues."

"Do you think she knew that someone wanted to kill her?"

"I'm not sure yet. Her murder was so violent I am sure it was a crime of passion. Somebody was angry at her, violently angry. Whether they planned it, I'm not sure. Whether she expected it? I doubt it. Not a year in advance. But she could have known that someone was angry at her."

I continued to look at what Chief had sorted into the "not relevant" pile. The box of books that Brenda had brought seemed important to me, but the chief had discounted them. I thought there might have been a message in one of them that would have been helpful.

"You're right," he said, "but to find anything important, we'd need time to go through every book, which I haven't had a chance to do yet. Maybe we could do that today."

I moved over to look at the "relevant" pile. I saw how important books were to my mother, because in that pile were books that I thought must have come from her book club. Those were the ones with the attendance list of names. I had noticed that Brenda's name was not on the list in any book.

Last in the relevant pile was the appointment calendar. I agreed with the chief on this one for relevance, especially because there were pages torn out of the book. Would the murderer have torn them out and thrown them away? "What do you think?" asked the chief.

"If we could find those pages or what else happened on those days to track down who she saw, that would be very helpful. I've seen detective shows where they lightly run a pencil over the page to see if the pen used by the person had left an impression."

I grabbed a pencil from the desk and lightly shaded the page.

And written there, in my mother's handwriting, was "Book Club–7:00." I showed the chief.

"That looks innocuous to me," he replied. "Why would somebody tear out those pages?"

"I don't know. Maybe my mother tore them out herself. Maybe the murderer tore them out. Have you ever talked to any of the people from the book club?"

"Until you brought these books to me, I didn't have any idea about the book club or the names of those who belonged. Let me look at the lists again, Mari."

Chief Langdon looked at the lists. Then he went to his laptop and started to Google the names. When we compared the lists, we found five women who belonged to the group, not counting my mother. Of those he Googled, three had died since then. Most of the members were an older group of women and the deaths were from natural causes. The last two had moved to warmer climates.

"I'll contact these last two and see what I can find out," he said. "But I think this is a good clue."

Finally, a good clue, something that we could work with (maybe!) I felt like jumping up and down, but I let my stomach do it for me while I sat still.

I went back to the box of books that Brenda had brought me. Mostly mysteries but tucked in among them was a thin book of poetry, *Sonnets from the Portuguese* by Elizabeth Barrett Browning. I looked through it, then I noticed there was a ribbon attached to the book that was used to mark a page. I used the ribbon to open the book and it opened to a page titled "Sonnet XLIII." Forty-three? Is this the XLIII on my locket? The house number 43? I read the poem. It was a very emotional proclamation of the poet's love, beginning, "How do I love thee, let me count the ways." I read the poem and when I got to the last line highlighted in yellow, "I shall but love thee better after death." I wondered if that was a premonition. My mother wore the locket all the time, even on the day they killed her. Her own grandmother and mother, who weren't murdered, passed the locket down to her. But in my mother's case, she had told my dad she wanted me to have it. Was it just a case of passing on an heirloom? But then why would she highlight that line, "I shall but love thee better after death?" Did she know?

I showed the book to Chief Langdon with the page, the poem, and its highlighted last line. "Do you think she knew?" My eyes filled with tears. If she knew, would the idea terrify her every day until it happened? Was there somebody she suspected? Someone who made her afraid every time she saw them? Was she being stalked by a violent murderer?

"Since this number was important to the women in your family and went back all those years, I don't believe that the number 43 was a special number to your mother outside of the locket. Maybe it had a special significance for your grandmother and great-grandmother and your mother was hunting for a reason for that and just found Elizabeth what's her name's poem and made it significant to you differently. Listen, Mari. I know you're upset so I'll give you a few minutes while I get us some tea."

Chief Langdon left the room and headed downstairs. Buddy came over and sat next to me the way he did the first day I met him, his big, brown dog eyes looking up at me. I put my hand on his head and slid it down into his thick German Shepherd fur. I thought of Emily's dog, Max, and remembered how every time I buried my hands in Max's fur it calmed me and made me less anxious. My reaction to Buddy was no different, and he put his big paws on my lap and raised his head to lick my tears away. I put my arms around his neck and rubbed his ears and buried my face in his thick fur. "Thanks, Buddy. You're a good boy."

He returned to sitting, and the door opened and in walked the chief with two cups of steaming hot tea and some cookies. The tea warmed my hands in the same way that the chief's kindness to me warmed my heart and inspired me to move on toward my goal of solving this terrible crime. When the chief sat down, Buddy stood up and went back to his bed but he kept watching me, his dark brown muzzle resting on his paws and if I didn't know any better, it looked like he had a worried look on his face.

"Buddy is such a great dog," I said. "He's so sweet."

"Yes, he is, but if we needed him to protect us, he'd know exactly what to do."

We combed through each of the books from the book club box. Occasionally there was a notation in pencil, but none of the notes seemed relevant to my mother's murder or showed that she had any kind of fear of anyone or anything. By that time, it was time for lunch and Chief Langdon suggested we go out to a little restaurant in town. It was decorated for Christmas with a big live wreath on the door and tiny white lights around the window frames. Each table had a small vase in the center with a poinsettia and a sprig of holly. We found a booth away from the door and settled in. The waitress, wearing an elf cap, came to take our order. Christmas music played softly in the background.

"Hi Chief," she said. "What can I get you two?"

We gave her our orders and resumed our conversation.

"Have we reached a dead end?" I asked.

"Not exactly," said the chief. "I still need to get in touch with the two remaining women from the book club, and I'll get on that."

"What do you think they'd tell you?"

"People in book clubs can get close. Depending on the books they're reading and discussing, they might share things from books that they can relate to in their own lives. One of those women might have some worthwhile information for us."

"Maybe I could do that instead." I offered. Chief agreed to let me make the calls.

Chief Langdon was well known in town, and as we ate, people stopped by to say hello. He introduced me using my full name, Mari Franklin. People were polite and smiled and wished us a Merry Christmas. But one man asked, "Is this…?"

"Yes, she is, Bill." Chief turned to me and said, "Bill worked with me on the police force. He was around when your mother died."

I smiled and shook his hand.

"It's good to see you all grown up," he said, and then he turned to the chief and said, "I'll call you after the holidays, Chief. Maybe we can get together."

"Sounds good." And Bill left.

Chief looked uncomfortable.

"What's the problem?' I asked.

"He won't wait until after the holidays. I'll bet I get a call tonight."

I think I knew why the Chief was upset, but I asked anyway.

"He'll only want to poke his nose into this and I don't want him around. I've been working on the case for fifteen years and you're committed to finding your mother's murderer, but he'll see it as something to play with, not as a genuine commitment like we do."

We finished lunch and left. We had barely gotten into the car when the chief's cell rang.

"Hi Bill. I knew you'd call, but I thought we said after the holidays. I need to put you on speakerphone."

Bill replied, "What's going on, Chief? Why is the girl here?" The chief motioned me to be quiet. I don't think Bill even heard him mention the speaker phone.

"She wanted info on her mother's murder, that's all."

"I thought you were done with that case, Chief. It was what... fifteen years ago?"

"The case was never closed. I work on it when I can."

"Chief, you need to let it go, sell that house and move to Florida like other retired people."

"Not yet. I need to finish this one. I'll see you around town. Merry Christmas." And he hung up.

Chapter 37

As we drove back to the house, the chief and I talked about number 43 on the house. Was it a coincidence that the house was at that address? Maybe my parents looked at a few houses and the address made my mother decide on this one? Maybe she saw it as an excellent omen. We walked past the number and through the front door where Buddy greeted us with his wagging tail. He led us upstairs to the office and planted himself in the dog bed with a deep sigh. Chief and I sat opposite each other. He became silent, looked down at the floor and rubbed his chin.

"Mari, I know you were very young when this happened, what was it, you were less than three years old, so this is a long shot, but have you ever tried to remember what happened that day?"

"I've tried a lot, but no luck. I've had a few dreams, but that's it."

"Tell me about the dreams. What did you see?"

"Not a lot. Just my house and someone coming up the driveway. I think it was a man, but I can't be sure. I've had the dream twice, the same dream, but when the person gets near the house, I wake up."

"I wonder about trying something. What would you say about being hypnotized?"

"I don't know. Why would I do that?"

"Maybe a hypnotherapist could bring you back to that day and help you remember it. Your memories might bring up more clues."

"Who would do it?"

"There's a psychologist I know who does hypnosis, and I told her about you. She offered to see you and speak to you about it, and maybe, if it seems appropriate, she could try it with you."

"Do you think it would help?"

"She will tell you if it wouldn't. Let me call her."

He picked up his cell phone and quickly called her number from his contact list.

"Hi, Dr. Adams. This is Chief Langdon. I have Mari Franklin here. She has some questions for you."

He handed me his phone. Her name was Dr. Danita Adams. She told me she was a licensed psychologist specializing in hypnotherapy. She had worked with teens for about ten years and had a great reputation as a psychologist working in the African American community. Her reputation had spread, and she opened a practice specializing in hypnotherapy. She agreed to see me that afternoon. Chief Langdon drove me to her office located in a modern office building near the hospital.

Chapter 38

"Hi, Chief Langdon. Good to see you again. So good to meet you, Mari," she said. She had a gentle, warm voice, and welcomed me into her office. Chief picked a chair in the waiting room.

"Can the chief come in with me?" I asked. "Just in case I remember something important." She agreed that it was ok, offered me a large, soft recliner to sit in, and sat across from me.

"Mari, tell me why you're here," she said as she leaned forward in her chair.

"You know that somebody murdered my mother when I was a baby. Chief Langdon and I have been working together on finding the killer, and he wondered if hypnosis would help me remember if I saw the murderer that day. Do you think it might?"

"It might. No guarantees, though. Do you know anything about hypnosis?"

"Just what I've seen on TV. What's it like, really?"

"I'll give you some directions to help you gradually go into a state of deep relaxation so you can become very open to suggestions. It's used to help women control pain during childbirth, or it can help people control unwanted behaviors like smoking, or anxiety, and sometimes it can help with the memory of certain events. With you, it might not work because the event was so traumatic, and you were so young. Hypnosis helps you with things you are willing to see or change, but if you don't want to go there, you won't. When you are under hypnosis, you are aware of what's going on around you. Some people become hyper-aware, hearing noises outside the room, for example."

"How long will it take?"

"It will take as long as it takes. But before we try it, I need to give you a few exercises to see how suggestible you are."

As I sat in the recliner, she asked me to close my eyes and she gave me a few directions to see how hypnotizable I was. When she asked me to open my eyes. She was smiling.

"You did very well, Mari. I think this might work if you want to try."

"I'll do it if it'll help find the killer."

"I can't guarantee that, but we can try. If you're ready, start by relaxing into the chair."

I slid back into the seat, and Dr. Adams, in her quiet, soothing voice, guided me into a hypnotic state. I was very relaxed but very aware of her voice that led me back in time three years ago, five years ago, ten years ago, all the way back to the day my mother was murdered. She re-created the day for me in slow, relaxing descriptions:

"Mari, I'm taking you back to the night before they murdered your mother. It's bedtime for you, around 7:30 in the evening. You are in your pajamas. Do you remember anything about going to bed?"

"I sort of remember my mother sitting with me in her rocking chair, holding me and reading a bedtime story. She covered both of us with a pink blanket."

"And then what happened?"

"I was very sleepy. My mother kissed me and put me in my bed, and I guess I fell asleep."

"Do you remember hearing anything as you were falling asleep?"

"I don't remember anything." My voice sounded very soft and far away as I answered Dr. Adams. I was very relaxed but very focused

on this experience.

"Do you remember waking up during the night?"

"No, I don't think so."

She continued, *"Let's go to the morning. Now you are waking up."*

"It's very dark."

"Is someone coming to wake you?"

"I think somebody is with me, but I don't know who."

I could feel myself frowning, almost like squeezing my brain trying hard to remember, but I couldn't remember anything. Dr. Adams spoke to me again.

"Relax and breathe," she said in her soothing voice. *"That's ok, Mari. Now, do you hear anything?" she asked.*

"No," I said. And I tried harder to remember. *"Wait, I can hear someone,"* I said. *"Someone is on the stairs…someone is in the hall. It's very dark…very dark. I can't see, but I hear a loud noise coming from my mom's room."* I was having trouble catching my breath. *"Somebody is hurting her, but I don't know who. It's too dark! The door is shut. I'm afraid that the person who is hurting my mother will find me. I need to hide."*

I was feeling terrified. I wanted to end this right now. Dr. Adams took over quickly with her reassuring voice.

"OK, Mari. I want you to relax. Breathe slowly. It's ok for you to come out of hypnosis. Keep breathing and wake up. Take your time. When you wake up, you'll feel relaxed and refreshed. You'll remember everything that happened, but you won't be afraid."

I woke up slowly, opened my eyes and my breathing slowed down. I was glad to be back to today. Dr. Adams told me to stay in the chair and relax for a while. I closed my eyes; I was feeling drained. I wasn't sure I could get out of the chair, anyway. Dr. Adams sat nearby, observing me. I looked at her clock. We had started the session forty-five minutes ago, but it felt like only a few minutes had passed.

"Did I have anything that we could use?" I asked, looking from her face to Chief Langdon's. He had a very serious look, very intense.

"Some details, but not a lot of specifics. It was early, it was dark and hard to see what was happening. You did hear a lot, and that could be very helpful." said the chief. "You said you heard someone coming up the stairs to your parents' room. That meant that the murderer wasn't someone already upstairs. Your father would have left for work earlier. If what you could remember was accurate, that might show that someone came into the house after he left and went upstairs to kill your mother."

"But you said 'if' what I said was accurate. Why wouldn't it be?"

Dr. Adams smiled and said, "Mari, you were so little. It's something that you and Chief should keep in mind, and maybe when what you remember gets put together with other evidence it will help. We could try again tomorrow. Maybe you could provide more information in another session."

"I would like to try," I said, and she and I agreed on a morning session.

I got out of the recliner. "Thanks," I said. The chief shook her hand, and we headed for the door.

Dr. Adams handed me her business card saying, "Mari, if you have questions, don't be afraid to call me. I'll see you tomorrow. You too, Chief."

Chapter 39

The mid-afternoon sun was bright and perked up my spirits. Connecticut sun shines regularly even in the winter, unlike the drab skies in Upstate New York where the sun hides from November to April. I could easily live here. I texted Jake, who told me he was home. Chief Langdon drove us back to his house on Windthorne Road, let me out of the car, and pulled it into the single garage. Using the entrance from the garage, the chief went into the house to make some notes on what had happened that afternoon and let the dog out. I crossed the driveway to Jake and Brenda's house and rang the doorbell. The nosey neighbor was at the front window in the house across the street. Creepy. Jake opened the front door and invited me into the kitchen. I pulled out a chair at the kitchen table opposite him. There was a pretty Christmas plate of decorated home-made cookies on the table wrapped in plastic wrap.

"How's it going?" asked Jake. "Anything new at all?"

"A few things. Dr. Adams hypnotized me today and even though I had no blockbuster clues to offer, the Chief thought it was helpful."

"Hypnotized? What's that supposed to do?" he asked.

"It's supposed to help me remember," I said.

"What was it like to be hypnotized?"

"It surprised me. I thought it would be like a weird, far away experience, but I was just very, very relaxed and I knew where I was. I guess it was like starting to fall asleep. Hard to explain. But I felt very good when I came out of it."

"I'm glad you're ok. What's next?"

"I'm going back tomorrow morning to try again."

Jake's phone rang. It was Brenda suggesting that we get a pizza and invite Chief Langdon for dinner. Jake ordered the pizza and called him. Chief asked if Buddy could come, and Jake said he was sure it would be okay with his mother. She arrived home shortly, followed by Chief Langdon and Buddy, and we gathered around the table with the red tablecloth to eat our pizza. Brenda asked what we had found out today.

"We have a few additional things, but nothing huge. We're trying hypnosis to take me back to that day to see what I remember."

Brenda's eyes looked up from her plate like someone looking over the top of her reading glasses.

"Is that reliable?" she asked.

"Dr. Adams says it can sometimes bring back memories that happened a long time ago. I remembered some things that happened that morning."

Brenda took a drink of red wine from her glass and looked back down at her plate.

"What could you possibly remember? You were a baby."

"I remembered sounds mostly, but I'm going back tomorrow to see if I can remember more things."

Brenda got up to get the plate of Christmas cookies and left for a few minutes. We moved to the family room and sat in front of the fire. There were two stockings hanging from the mantle, one labeled "Jake" and the other labeled "Brenda." Next to the fireplace was an artificial tree trimmed with colored lights and ornaments. A few gifts were under the tree.

We finished most of the Christmas cookies as we sat in front of the fire. Buddy, who usually sat at my feet, wandered around the room sniffing as he went.

Jake got up and said, "Come on, Buddy. Let's go find you something to play with." He headed for the basement with the dog padding along behind him. The dog's nails clicked on the wooden stairs that creaked a little with the weight of both. Then it sounded like Jake was rummaging around in the basement. When the rummaging stopped, both returned to the group, but Buddy had a stuffed animal in his mouth and a tail wagging a mile a minute.

"Pupster!" Brenda said. "Where did you find him?" Her eyes were wide with surprise.

"He was in a box full of my stuff downstairs."

"What is a Pupster?" I asked.

"He was my favorite toy. Mom made him for me when I was a little guy. How old was I, Mom?"

"I think you were about three," she said, her voice becoming low as she looked intently at Buddy chewing and licking old Pupster. You'd think it was a piece of steak. "You don't want Buddy to have this, Jake, do you?" As she reached down to take it away from him, Buddy let out a low growl and put his paws down hard on the stuffed animal. Brenda pulled her hand back quickly.

"I guess you don't need it anymore, Jake," I said. We all laughed as Buddy held the toy in his front paws, licked it and chewed on it.

"Looks like it's Buddy's toy now," said Chief Langdon.

"Right," said Jake, laughing. "A soggy, chewed Pupster doesn't interest me at all."

The three of us, Buddy, Chief and I, left and when we got outside, I turned and said to Chief Langdon, "I'll see you tomorrow morning. Thanks so much for your hard work and for being with me today."

"That's okay. We'll solve this." His voice sounded determined, and I knew he was right. After the chief went in the house, Jake and I got in my car to talk about his father. Jake wanted reassurance that I hadn't told Emily or anyone else about his father being alive and living in Upstate New York.

"Jake," I said, "I promised you and I'd never go back on that, not even to Emily. I told you I'm planning to see your father soon, and when I do, I'll let you know all about it. Did you hear any more from him?"

"Yes, but nothing new. He's a little nervous about seeing you, afraid that his secret will come out."

"What secret?"

"He disappeared 15 years ago and now is in touch with me and not with my mother. That's an enormous deal, don't you think?'

"Oh yeah," I said. But I thought, "I want to hear the story, so believe me, I'll be visiting him. I'm nervous about it too. Maybe he's the murderer and maybe I'm next."

Chapter 40

The next morning, I drove to Dr. Adams' office, where Chief Langdon was waiting outside. As we walked in, I could smell coffee brewing in one office on her floor. She greeted us and we went into her inner office, and I immediately went to the recliner, eager to get started.

"How are you feeling today, Mari? Did you sleep well?"

I had a very restless night, full of snippets of dreams about my mother. Some were scary and upsetting. I wondered if it was because of the hypnosis, so I asked.

"Sometimes, like in your situation, when there's trauma involved, the brain processes what is going on during sleep. It may not be pleasant. This may continue while you are working on the murder, and it may last beyond that time. It can be a tough time for you, Mari. We can stop these sessions if you find it too difficult."

"No," I said. "I need to go on."

I slipped into a hypnotic state more easily than I did yesterday, back to my bedroom and my bed on that morning in February.

"OK Mari let's go back to your bed. It's very early in the morning. What do you see?"

"It's very dark. I can't see much."

"Is anybody in your room with you?"

"Somebody. I don't know. Somebody is next to my bed."

"Can you tell if it's a man or a woman?"

"Not really. I want to say it's a man because the person seems tall."

"Ok. And can you tell what the person is wearing?"

"No. It's too dark."

"Can you smell anything?"

"Yes. It smells like toothpaste."

"Toothpaste?"

"Like somebody is ready to go to work. I think the person by my bed is my dad. I think he just put something next to me in my bed."

"What did he put in your bed, Mari?"

"I don't know. I think I fell asleep."

"When you woke up, did you hear anything or see anything?"

"It was still dark, but I heard that noise from my mother's room."

"Tell me about the noise you heard coming from her room. What did it sound like?"

"A thud. Something heavy hitting something else."

"Did you see anything else?"

"My door is opening. Somebody is peeking in at me. Somebody with a white hat on, I think. I'm so scared."

"Can you see anything else?"

"No. They closed the door. I'm still terrified, but I hear them closing the door to my room."

"It's okay, Mari. Is there anything else?"

"I hear somebody in my mother's room, I think. I hear someone moving around in there. They are doing something, but I don't know…I'm so scared."

I turned onto my side in the chair and tried to curl up, hugging myself and trying to make myself invisible. Then I heard Dr. Adams' voice.

"Mari, you don't have to stay there if you're frightened. You can come back whenever you want."

I began to open my eyes, wanting to wake up. Dr. Adams continued to speak.

"Take some deep breaths and open your eyes. Everything is okay.

You're safe."

I slowly opened my eyes all the way and saw Dr. Adams and Chief Langdon. My hands were shaking, but slowly I felt safe again. Dr. Adams brought me a glass of water.

"You did great, Mari," she said.

"Yes, you did," said the Chief. "I think we have some more helpful information to go on."

It took me a few minutes of sitting in the soft recliner until I felt calm enough to get up.

When I did, I got up slowly. Dr. Adams stayed with me until I felt ok about leaving. She walked me to the door and said goodbye to both of us. I was feeling a little drained.

Chief Langdon and I went back to his house. We sorted out what we already had for clues, but the most important clues came from the hypnosis. If what I remembered was true, my dad came into my room before the murder and was ready for work. He put something in my bed–probably a bottle or a Sippy cup to help me go back to sleep until my mother got up. But after he left, there was somebody else there. The noise that I heard could have been the murderer or the murder happening. Then I heard more noise that could have been the clean-up. The killer peeked into my room and was wearing a white hat. Why the white hat?

Chapter 41

The chief wanted to talk a little about what was in the boxes I brought, but he also wanted to know what my thoughts were about the stuff in the attic.

"Nothing else sticks in my mind. Maybe the towels..."

"What towels?" he asked.

"There was a set of monogrammed towels, blue, with an "F" embroidered on them. One of the two big towels was missing, but the hand towels and facecloths were all in the box. I asked Grandma if she knew what happened to the missing towel. She didn't know, she guessed that it might have been in the wash when we packed up and moved."

Chief Langdon put his elbow on the desk and rested his chin in his hand. He closed his eyes. "Hmm," he said.

Then I had an idea. "Maybe the murderer took it to clean up. They could have raided the laundry closet to find the towel. Then they could have taken it to keep the police from finding it," I said, "And that's why the murder scene was so clean."

"Now you're thinking like an investigator," Chief said.

"Chief, I'd like to try one more hypnosis session. Do you think Dr. Adams would be available tomorrow?"

"I can ask." And he called her office and set up another appointment.

The next morning, I slid one more time into the leather recliner and relaxed as I listened to Dr. Adams' voice. I was hypnotized within minutes.

"Mari let's go back to your bedroom. You are in your bed. Your dad has left for work. Do you hear or see anything?"

"Yes. I hear a noise in my mother's room. Someone is hurting her. Now I see someone in a white hat looking into my room."

"Tell me about the hat, Mari. What kind of hat is it?"

I tried hard to focus, to concentrate on the person in the doorway.

"It's not a baseball hat. It's close to their head, like a hoodie."

"OK. That's good. Can you go a little deeper into hypnosis?"

I relaxed more and felt my breathing slowing.

"I hear a voice. The person in the hoodie is talking to me. They're whispering… 'It's over, Sweetie, but I'll be back.' And then they closed the door. I hear them going down the steps, leaving me. When are they coming back? Are they coming back to hurt me? I'm all alone and I'm so scared. Why doesn't my mother come to take care of me? I crawled under the bed to hide, and I think I fell asleep on the floor. I needed to stay there in case the bad person came back."

"OK Mari. I know that this is hard for you. You can come back from hypnosis. You'll feel relaxed when you wake up and you'll remember everything."

I woke up and reviewed it all in my head. Who was the person in the white hoodie? I felt relaxed and Dr. Adams asked if I felt OK. She told me to sit for a while until I got my composure back. After a few minutes, I got up, and she hugged me and looked carefully at me to make sure I was alright.

"You did great, Mari. I hope this was helpful. Chief, I hope it was helpful to you, too."

Chief Langdon and I looked at each other and nodded in agreement.

Chapter 42

Jake was home when we got back to Windthorne, and he suggested we go for a walk. We asked Chief Langdon if we could take Buddy with us. We wanted to go to a nearby park where we could talk, and Buddy could get some exercise.

"Let's go, Buddy," Jake said. The dog jumped into my car with Pupster, his new favorite toy, in his mouth.

The park ran along the shore of a small lake and Buddy bounded out of the car and dropped Pupster at my feet, looking to play fetch. After a few throws, he abandoned the toy and went off to play with another dog. Jake and I sat on a bench to talk.

"Have you heard any more from your father?" I asked.

"He's OK. He's waiting to see you when you get back."

"I hope he has something to tell me that'll help."

"Mari, he's willing to meet with you so that makes me think he does. Have you and the chief gotten any closer to solving the murder?"

"Dr. Adams was very helpful. I think we're getting close. Chief Langdon has been great. He's such a smart guy, and he's really been working on this for so long. He made a genuine commitment to this case a long time ago. But I have my theory, which I haven't shared with anyone yet, and don't plan to until I'm sure of who the murderer is."

"You haven't even shared it with Emily?" he laughed.

"Nope. Nobody. Not until I'm sure. Do you have anything that you want me to bring to your dad? How about if I take a picture of you for him in front of your house?"

"Sounds good," he said. We called Buddy back to the car. He picked up Pupster and jumped into the back seat. I drove back to Windthorne where I took Jake's picture along with that big, happy German Shepherd with a stuffed toy in his mouth. One last dinner at Brenda and Jake's house. Just me and them. Chief had a meeting and couldn't come. But the nosy neighbor was watching as I arrived, and his curtains fluttered as usual.

We talked about nothing really. I was trying to keep away from discussing the murder or accidentally mentioning Jake's father. We talked about the weather, the drive to Rochester and school until it was time to go. I was leaving in the morning, so I wished them a Merry Christmas and thanked Brenda for providing me with dinner while I was in town.

"Merry Christmas to your family, too." She said. "Stay in touch. I'll be working all week, but if you need anything, just call me."

Jake walked me to the car.

"Thanks for everything, Jake. I'll get back to you about your dad. You know, I wanted to ask your mother, but I forgot–where does she work?"

"She owns her own cleaning business."

Chapter 43

The next morning, Chief Langdon and I met for one more time in the hotel dining room for breakfast.

"Have you come to any conclusions about the murder?" he asked.

"I think I'm close Chief, but I want to be sure before I tell you what I think."

"We can still brainstorm it, Mari."

"I want to do that, but I just want to wait a little longer. I also need to call the two women from the book club."

"Okay. I know we both want to solve this, and I'm eager to see what you've got, and if your opinion matches mine. That's all."

I told him, "I have one more thing to do before I can put everything together. When I get that done, I think we'll be ready to make some conclusions."

I couldn't tell him that the last thing on my list was to meet with Greg Henderson, Jake's dad.

"I really need to get going," I said, and gave him a hug and headed for my car.

"Drive safely, Mari."

"Thanks, Chief. I'll talk to you soon."

I welcomed the sound of the ignition as I turned the key. Waving goodbye, I headed back toward Rochester. Grandpa had satellite radio in his car, and I turned on the Totally Christmas station so I could distract myself by singing along with Christmas carols. But it didn't work. My mind went back to the hypnosis sessions, especially the last one. I was trying to focus on the person in the white hood. Their body, the way they moved, was at the center of my focus. And the voice. The whisper. *"It's over, Sweetie, but I'll be back."* Haunting. Familiar. Was there genuine affection in that voice? Was it sarcasm? Who was it?

I kept driving and thinking, and next thing I knew I was in Syracuse where I stopped for a fast-food lunch. I called home and when Grandma answered I told her I'd be there in about ninety minutes.

"I'm glad you'll be home soon," she said. "I'm waiting to bake Christmas cookies with you. The dough is chilling in the fridge."

"Grandma, that's one of our best traditions," I said. And I meant what I said. I could feel myself smiling. We had done Christmas baking ever since I was little. This murder was weighing so heavily on me I wished I could go back to being a little girl again with nothing to worry about except if I had been good enough so Santa would bring me what I asked for. "See you in a little while."

I threw away the trash from my lunch and got back in the car. The songs on the radio started as soon as I started the ignition. This time I was getting into the holiday spirit, and I sang Christmas carols all the way home.

I pulled into the driveway and Grandpa and Grandma came out to meet me. Grandpa unloaded my suitcase from the trunk. The boxes I had brought with clues were on the back seat, and we left them until later. We went inside to the family room that Grandma had decorated for Christmas. The tree was up, and our stockings hung from the mantle, draped with evergreen boughs cut from the bottom of the tree harvested from Grandma's woods. A large red candle surrounded by a natural wreath was on the coffee table, and around the room were other decorations that my grandparents put out every year. Santa's reindeer, angels. You name it; they saved it and used it every year.

It was good to have these traditions and decorations that were a part of my life for as long as I could remember. I walked around the room and picked up each object and looked at my family's history. I was happy to be home. I sat down and relaxed into the couch.

"Tell us about your trip, Mari," said Grandpa.

"It was so interesting. I learned so much."

"I'm glad you're home," he said. He held me close and for a long time. That was different, too. Was it the Christmas spirit or did something happen while I was gone?

I told them about my visit with Chief Langdon, but I left out a lot of details about things we looked at and talked about. I told them he had lots of information about the murder, but I didn't tell them about his office. I had decided not to tell them about the hypnosis sessions. Not yet anyway.

Then Emily dropped by. "Hi. I saw the car was back. How was the trip?"

"Let's go upstairs to my room," I said. "I'll give you the Jake report if you give me the Seth report."

It was so good to be home with everyone, to get ready to celebrate the holidays, and to see Em. I was looking forward to seeing Seth and spending quality time with him. Em and I talked about Seth and Jake, what we had gotten them for Christmas and what our plans were for the holidays. I told Em I wasn't ready to talk about my trip to Danbury yet, but eventually I'd have a lot to tell her. My phone beeped. It was a text from Seth. He wanted to go out to see the Christmas lights tonight.

Chapter 44

Seth looked amazing. He was glad to see me and immediately kissed me and took my hand as we walked through downtown. I was the happiest I'd been in a long time. We walked around the area to see the houses all decorated for the holidays Seth put his arm around me and I felt warm and secure. The lights were brighter than they seemed in other years. Maybe it was being in love, maybe it was feeling like I was close to finding my mother's murderer. Probably it was the combination of both. Life was so good at that moment.

The day before Christmas, Em, Jodi, Nicole, and I got together at my house to exchange presents and celebrate a little. They asked about my trip, and I gave them the short version. I wanted to celebrate with them. I didn't want to spend the holiday talking about murder, and I told them that. Besides, I needed to save my energy for the meeting with Jake's dad. My friends and I hung out, baked cookies with my grandmother, decorated them with all kinds of frosting and colored sugar, and ate the cookies. We laughed a lot and enjoyed ourselves. Grandma sat down at the piano and started playing Christmas songs and we all began to sing. Surprisingly, even Dad and Grandpa joined in.

On Christmas morning, Grandma woke me up, just like she had done since I was little. I could smell cinnamon buns and bacon and eggs, a perfect Christmas breakfast. After breakfast we went to open presents, and everyone got the usual sweaters, socks and candy. Stockings were filled with soap, Chapstick, hand cream and candy canes. Our traditional gifts. I loved this day.

But today was a little different. I didn't get my usual sweater. Instead, my grandfather gave me a small box.

"Jewelry?" I asked.

"Just open it," Dad said. "It's from all of us."

I opened the box and there, wrapped in red tissue and lying in green shredded paper was the key to a car!

"Oh, wow!" I said. "My own car! Where is it?"

Grandma laughed, "It's probably outside. We couldn't fit it in here."

I ran to the front window and looked out. In the driveway was a small, blue SUV.

I couldn't believe it! Not having to ask to use anybody else's car! OMG! I could hardly believe it.

"It's not brand-new, but it's only two years old with very low mileage. We want you to be safe now and when you go to college."

"Dad, Grandma and Grandpa, it's beautiful. Thank you so much. Can I take it for a drive?"

"Sure," Grandma laughed, "But you'd better change out of your nightgown and bathrobe before you leave!"

It took me about five minutes to run upstairs and change. I texted Seth and Em to look out their window to see the car and they came over to get a closer look.

"Congratulations, Mari, Merry Christmas. Nice car!"

"Isn't it great?" I said. "I'm so happy because now I don't need to rely on anybody else to get around."

"You got to love that taste of freedom," Seth said.

"And that new car smell," Em said.

Oh yes. They must have had a special spray for that since it wasn't a brand-new car.

"Get in and we'll go for a ride."

Em said, "You guys go. I'm sure you want to be alone. I'm going to help Mom with Christmas dinner."

Seth and I drove out to the lake, pulled into the parking lot, and he turned to me and kissed me. Then he took a small, wrapped box out of his pocket, gave it to me and said, "Merry Christmas, Mari."

I opened the box, and there was a silver bracelet, very plain and very pretty.

"Thanks, Seth. It's perfect. I love it. Help me put it on." He gently slid the bracelet around my wrist and fastened it. I kissed him. Then I reached into my bag for his gift. I knew how important his college was to him, so I had ordered a thick, warm scarf from the college to keep him warm as he walked from building to building for his classes on campus.

"This is perfect too," he smiled. "Thanks, Mari."

He kissed me again and we stayed there for a while. It had started to snow. Maybe we will have a romantic white Christmas this year. It was a perfect moment. We sat for a while just enjoying being together, holding hands and kissing. It seemed like we hadn't been alone in a long time. But now it was time to get back home.

I drove us back, parked my new car, kissed Seth goodbye, and went home to help with Christmas dinner.

Chapter 45

The day after Christmas, I had two items on my list of things to do. First, I needed to call the two women from the book club, and then I needed to call Jake's dad.

The first woman I called had no information for me about my mother. I followed with a call to the second woman, Francine O'Neill.

"Mrs. O'Neill, my name is Mari Franklin. My mother was in your book club about 15 years ago."

"Mari, of course!" she said. "My goodness, you must be all grown up."

"Sort of, I guess. I'm sure you know that my mother's murderer was never found."

"Yes. That was such a terrible time for your family. All the book club members were devastated."

"Mrs. O'Neill, do you remember anything about that time that could help?"

"No, I don't. But my brother-in-law Phil might. He's lived across the street for over 30 years. He's also nosey. If anyone knew anything it would be him. He's at my house for the holiday. Here, I'll get him, and you can ask."

I thought that I was lucky to find him there and I could talk to him over the phone instead of visiting him in his house.

I heard some conversation between the two, and then she handed the phone to him.

"Hello?" he said in an uncertain voice.

"Hi, Phil. This is Mari Franklin. You may have seen me visiting my old house on your street, the house owned by Chief Langdon. I've been working on solving my mother's murder and wondered if you remembered anything from that time that might be helpful to me."

"I saw you there, and I saw you next door at the Henderson's, too. What questions do you have?" he asked. "I was interviewed by the police back then, and I didn't have any information to offer them. I didn't see anything at all until the police arrived that night."

Given the number of times I noticed him looking out his front window, I was sure he had seen something. What was he hiding?

"What about in the days following the murder?" I asked, feeling impatient. I began to pace with the phone.

He started to sound defensive. "The Hendersons cleaned out the house and called Goodwill to take most of the stuff. Then after the house went on the market, they cleaned out what was left for the trash collectors. Nobody wanted what was left so it got thrown away."

"There must have been some good stuff that the Hendersons put out for the trash collector. In my neighborhood at home, people drive around on trash collection day looking for stuff that they can take, like furniture or other stuff."

"Nooo," he said slowly. "The furniture was all taken by Goodwill, but I did find a couple of things myself."

"Like what?' I asked, starting to gesture wildly with my non-phone hand as I got more impatient.

"A couple of almost-full cans of paint and a white hazmat suit to wear while I'm painting or doing hazardous work, like putting in insulation. I thought it would come in handy. The suits aren't expensive at all, but it's convenient to have one." He laughed a little. "I never used it. I think I still have it in the basement."

I tried not to jump up and down with excitement. "Phil," I said, "Can you try not to handle it too much, put it in a plastic bag and save it for me or Chief Langdon?"

"Am I in trouble?" he asked. "It was in the trash pile. It's not like I stole it."

"No, you're not in trouble. Just hold on to it for me and don't let anyone else have it except the chief. When will you be home?"

"Tomorrow morning."

I called Chief Langdon and told him about the hazmat suit. He agreed to stop by Phil's house to pick it up for testing.

Chapter 46

Next on my agenda was calling Jake's father. Jake had told him to expect my call, and he answered on the second ring. We set up a time to meet the next afternoon at the church office where he worked. When I got there, I parked on the street in front of the office behind a pickup truck that I figured was his. I rang the doorbell. The door was opened by an older woman.

"Merry Christmas," she said with a warm smile. "You must be Mari."

"I am. Merry Christmas."

"Hi. I'm Julia, the church secretary. Greg is in the room down the hall."

She motioned for me to follow and took me to a small office. Jake's dad was waiting, standing in the middle of the room.

"Would you like some hot chocolate?" Julia asked.

"That would be great, thank you."

"Mari," he said, "Call me Greg. It's so good to see you. I'd know you anywhere. You look just like your mother."

"Thanks, Greg, that's what everyone says." I smiled, feeling great about that.

"By the way, here's a picture of Jake in front of his house," I said, showing him the picture on my phone. "He looks like you, too."

"Nobody knows you're here, right?" he said, smiling at

Jake's image.

"Only Jake," I said. "But I need to ask you why it's such a secret?"

"I left a long time ago. There was a lot of stress between Brenda and me. It got bad after your mother died. Whether losing your mother as a friend really affected her, I don't know. Brenda's personality went through a lot of changes. She was depressed, angry and she seemed to want to take it out on me. We fought constantly, and I decided it would be better for everyone if I left. Once I did, I didn't look back. But that's between me and her. Jake, I'm afraid, was collateral damage."

He left her and never sent her any child support for Jake. I began to feel sorry for Brenda, but at the same time I admired the strength she had in starting a business to support herself. No wonder she was angry at Greg, and everyone else for that matter. "Collateral damage?" Poor Jake. That was so cold. I was starting to dislike Greg a lot, but I still needed his help.

"Jake told me you're trying to solve the murder. I'm not sure I have anything helpful to tell you, but I can try. What do you need from me?"

"I wish you could tell me who did this to my mother. Maybe you can help me figure it out. Do you remember anything about that time? Oh, and do you mind if I record our conversation?"

"Yes, I do mind. Our meeting is supposed to be a secret." I put my phone away.

"It was fifteen years ago, Mari. Overall, your parents were good friends with us, although the friendship was really between Brenda and your mother because your dad and I were busy with work. We didn't have a lot of time for hanging out unless our wives insisted or if we ran into each other when we were in the yard."

"Brenda says that she and my mother were best friends. They used to walk around the neighborhood together with their strollers when Jake and I were babies."

"Yes, they did. Every morning during the week."

"Do you know what they talked about?"

"I'm sure they talked about being moms for the first time. Maybe they talked about me and your dad."

"Brenda said they talked about books a lot."

"Yup. They both read a lot. They were always lending books back and forth and when they went out with you and Jake, sometimes they walked to the library. They took you kids to a 'baby and mom' reading program."

"I never heard that," I said. "But it makes sense if they really liked to read, they'd want us to read, too. Did you know my grandparents?"

"I only met them a few times. I remember they used to come to Danbury about once a month just for the weekend to see you."

"Do you think they got along with my mother?"

"Hard to tell. I couldn't say because I wasn't around them that much."

The secretary returned with the hot chocolate. I took a noisy sip, then I asked Greg about Brenda. "Do you remember anything happening between my mother and Brenda?"

"At one point your mother met some women who had a book club. They used to meet on Thursday nights. Brenda couldn't go. Maybe your mother didn't invite her, maybe there was something else, maybe she was jealous of Marianne's new friends, but she got mad. She stopped talking to Marianne. Your mother even gave her some books they read after they finished discussing them, but that only made Brenda angrier. She looked out the window every Thursday to watch your mother leave. Anyway, I tried not to be around much on Thursdays. I stayed late at work when it was book club night. When I got home, Brenda was usually in bed. She was pretty much in a nasty mood well into the next day."

"Why was she so angry? I asked. "It seems like it's not such a big thing. They could still walk together and talk."

"Oh, but Brenda stopped the walks. She was so furious about Marianne's friends that she refused to walk with her in the mornings."

"Didn't Brenda have other friends?"

"Not really. At least nobody I knew. Like I said, after she broke up the friendship with your mother, she changed a lot. That was part of my reason for leaving. She stopped talking, and I got sick of the anger and the silence."

"Did my mother know about how upset Brenda was?"

"I think she tried to fix things, but it only made Brenda angrier."

"She told me my dad and I stayed with you guys that night."

"Yeah, you did. Your dad asked if we had room for your grandparents when they arrived the next day, but Brenda said they should go to a hotel. She said we didn't have room."

"And you sold our house to the chief?"

"I was the realtor. After the crime scene tapes came down, I arranged for Goodwill to come and take things away. Brenda helped me put some stuff aside for your father, and a lot was left at the curb for the trash collector. Then she cleaned the house before it went on the market. She had just started her cleaning business a few months before."

He went on, "The only thing left in the house was your mother's rocker. I saved it for your dad, but he didn't want it. When the chief bought the house, he asked me to leave the chair. Does he still have it?"

"Yes. He keeps it in the nursery."

"Weird." Greg said, shaking his head. "I thought it was strange that he wanted that house, anyway."

"I think he was determined to solve the murder, and maybe he needed a place to live and since it was a good price…" I shrugged my shoulders.

Then I asked him my enormous question, "Who do you think killed my mother?"

"I don't know. I have no actual evidence to base anything on. All I can tell you it wasn't me."

I asked him if he would talk to Chief Langdon. It could be secret, just like our conversation.

"No. I know it'd get back to Brenda and I don't want to deal with her."

"But Greg, I need to tell Chief what you told me."

"That's your decision, but you promised that this would be between you and me."

"Finding my mother's killer is my primary goal. I need to break this promise."

Greg stood up, banging into the table. He knocked over our cups and stormed out. The secretary was on her way in to check on us and narrowly missed being knocked over, too. I apologized for the mess and dashed toward the door, chasing after Greg. I stepped outside, but he had disappeared. There was no sign of the pickup truck, either.

Chapter 47

Where did he go? I drove around the area looking, but there was no trace of him.

I went back into the office and found Julia.

"Julia," I said, "Greg left but I wasn't finished talking to him. How can I get in touch with him? Do you have his address?" There was a sense of panic in my voice.

Julia must have heard it, so she walked outside with me and gave me directions to Greg's farm. I thanked her and got into the car and set off down Route 5 and 20 looking for Greg. It took me about fifteen minutes to find the place and as I pulled into the gravel drive, I could see that his pickup truck wasn't there. Did I ruin my relationship with him, with Jake, and with Brenda and Chief Langdon? I hope not. I needed them all so I can solve this.

It was time to go home.

Driving back gave me time to think. Mom and Brenda were best friends, and then they weren't. How did that happen? Was that something that might happen to me and Emily? Would I ever do something that would cause Emily to get so angry with me that our friendship would be over? I don't think I would let that happen, at least I hoped not. Emily was so important to me. It sounded like Brenda was jealous of my mother's newly discovered friends. She wanted their friendship to stay the way it was. I wondered how my mother felt about the end of the friendship, but maybe she didn't think it was ending.

I thought about me and Em and what might happen to our friendship when she found out I'd been secretly texting with her boyfriend. I hadn't told her about the burner phone or his father. That was big. That might cause the end of my friendship with her. Probably Jodi and Nicole would take her side, and I wouldn't blame them. My mind was working overtime on this.

I pulled off into a rest stop and called Jake.

"Jake, I just met with your dad."

"How did it go? Did you learn anything?'

"Yes, I did. But your father got mad and left, and I have no idea where he went. I need to talk to Chief Langdon about this."

"No, you can't, you promised."

"This is too important, Jake. I'm breaking that promise. I'm going to talk with Chief Langdon."

"I need to call my dad."

"But he's gone, Jake. He left and he's not at home. I told him I needed to tell the Chief that he was around, and he ran away. Jake, wait. I need some time."

"For what?' Jake asked.

"I don't know," I said. "Maybe we can find him." And I hung up.

I decided that I had to tell Emily about Jake's father before she found out from anybody else.

I pulled into our driveway and sat for a minute to collect my thoughts. I could smell the fire in the fireplace. I went inside where Grandma was setting the table for dinner.

"Hi, honey, how was your trip? Did the car handle well?"

"I'm so glad to have the car, Grandma. It's the best gift ever."

"Where did you go, anyway? You were gone for a while."

"I drove down to Geneva just to try out the car."

"I'm surprised you didn't take Emily or Seth with you."

"I know, but I needed some time by myself to think."

Grandpa came into the kitchen and handed me what looked like a pile of rags.

"I brought the boxes that were in my car up to your room. I found this in the back seat."

"Thanks, Grandpa."

I looked closely at the rags and recognized Pupster, the toy that Jake gave to Buddy. Buddy must have left it in the back seat when we took him to the park and played fetch. The toy's stuffing, made from old rags, was falling out. Buddy did a wonderful job chewing him up in our game of fetch. I tried to put the stuffing back inside the toy, but the fabric wouldn't fit. I went up to my room to get a needle and thread to fix Pupster. I took the stuffing out to re-shape it and re-stuff the toy. That's when I saw it. A navy-blue monogram–F– on a piece of blue towel. The towel looked familiar, like the towels I found in the attic. Was this one of the missing towels? How did it get inside of Pupster? I knew where the towel came from.

I went down to the laundry room where Grandma had left all the linens we found upstairs, and on the top of the pile were the monogrammed hand towels. Same monogram as the piece of towel I found inside Pupster – same color, made by the same company. Brenda had said that she made the toy for Jake when he was about three years old. That was about the same time my mother was murdered. How did Brenda get the towel?

I emailed Chief Langdon with a picture of the piece of towel from the toy and pictures of the monogrammed hand towels. My phone rang almost immediately.

"Put the towels and Pupster in a safe place. Don't tell anyone what you found, and I'll get back to you soon," he said.

I didn't tell him anything about Jake's dad. I put everything in a plastic bag and hid it in the back of my closet. Then I headed over to Emily's house.

Chapter 48

"I need to talk to you, Emily," I said. "Can we go up to your room?" We climbed the stairs, went into her room and I sat in the comfy chair she had in the corner. Her dog Max climbed into my lap and made himself comfortable. Em sat on her bed, her back against the pillows, shoes off, getting settled in.

"What's going on? You seem too serious for somebody who just got a car for Christmas. You should be jumping up and down."

I looked at her seriously. "I need to tell you something important and I hope you won't be mad at me."

"Mari, we've been friends forever. Just tell me."

"Listen Em, Jake and I have a secret."

"You and Jake aren't in love or something, are you?" She sat up straight on the bed. I really had her attention.

"No, it's nothing like that. You're my best friend. I'd never do that to you, and besides, you know I'm in love with your brother."

"Whew," she said and sat back against the pillows.

"Jake's dad is alive. I've known it for a long time and I feel so bad about not telling you. Really.

"Wow!" she said, sitting up again. "How did you find out?"

"Jake heard from him and told me they've been in touch for a while. I talked to him myself. Get this, Em, he lives in Shortsville. He's only forty minutes away from here."

"Does Brenda know?"

"Not at all, and you can't tell her."

"I won't say a word. Does Jake know that you're telling me?"

"Yes. He does now. He didn't want me to tell anyone, not even you. I hope you're not mad at me. Here's the second part of this. I met with Jake's dad today."

Now Em was kneeling on the bed with her hands on the footboard.

"What? And what did you find out? Did he kill your mother?"

My eyes opened wide at her question. I guess she stunned me with how blunt she was, but then I knew she was asking the same question I wanted to ask Greg. She asked me where he was, and I told her I assumed he was still in Shortsville, but I wasn't sure.

"Did you tell Chief Langdon?"

"Not yet. I will though, for sure. I just know how protective Jake is about his dad. I also think Brenda will be furious at Jake and me for not telling her. She's already furious at Greg for leaving her and she's got fifteen years of anger stored up."

Then Em said, "Poor Jake. When's he going to tell his mother? Where does this leave him? Both his mother and father will be furious at him, his dad will be mad at you for telling and it will upset his mother that you knew about his dad and didn't tell her. I should call him right away."

"Well, you call him. I need to go home and think for a while and then call Chief Langdon." I left Emily sitting on the bed with her phone in her hand. I went home and went straight to my room and called Chief Langdon. No answer, so I left a message.

Chapter 49

I picked up the phone on the first ring. I knew it was the chief. I swallowed hard and told him about Jake's father, how he and Jake had been in touch, and how I texted with him. There was no response for a few seconds, then he asked, "Where is he?" I could hear tension in his voice. More than that. It seemed like he was trying hard not to explode.

"He's about forty minutes from Rochester. I went to see him."

"Why didn't you tell me about him? Did you go by yourself? Of course, you did," he sighed.

"Yes, but I met him in a church office. He works there as a handyman."

"Regardless, it wasn't a good idea. You could have been in danger. How can I get in touch with him?"

I gave him Greg's phone number.

"OK, I'll talk to you later."

Now that everything about my contact with Greg was out in the open, I was feeling relieved. At least I didn't have to tell Brenda. I'm sure she'll be totally upset that Jake and I knew about Greg, and I wondered who she'd be the maddest at. Poor Jake! I tried to call him, but there was no answer. He was probably talking to Emily. My dad and my grandparents were downstairs, so I decided I'd better let them know what was going on, too.

Everybody was sitting in front of the fire, so I joined them and began the conversation. "I need to tell you all what's been happening," I began. "We've found Jake's father."

The three of them looked up at me with a combination of shock and surprise on their faces.

"YOU found him?" Dad said.

"No. Actually, he and Jake have been in touch for a while. He agreed to talk with me, and I went to meet him. He only lives about forty minutes from here."

"That was risky, Mari. He could be the murderer."

"He's not, and honestly, I suspect everyone until there is a reason not to." I said.

"Who have you suspected?" Grandpa asked.

"Everyone, Grandpa, you not so much, but Dad and Grandma."

Dad said, "I can understand you suspecting me. Everybody thinks it was me, but Grandma? Really?"

"You did? Why? Why would you think it was me?" asked Grandma. She looked hurt. I never saw that look on her face before.

"You told me you and Mom weren't close. That you were unhappy with her marrying Dad, moving away, the album with no pictures of her, and the way you were chopping wood in the backyard. You were in Danbury the day before they killed her. You could have pretended to leave and then come the next morning to kill her."

Grandpa said, "Mari, I was with your grandma. She came home the day before and then we went back to Danbury as soon as we got the call from your dad. I can vouch for her. And then she stepped in to take care of you. She–no we–have loved you so much. She had nothing to do with your mom's murder." He sounded so hurt, too.

I felt guilty for suspecting Grandma. I should have talked more with her and with Grandpa. I believed everything Grandpa said, and I went to Grandma to hug her. She put her arms around me. We said nothing, we just held onto each other.

I was glad I made up with Grandma because I was thinking that maybe the chief was furious with me. A few minutes later, I heard a car pull into the driveway. Dad looked out the window to see who it was.

"What's he doing here?" Dad said.

There was a knock at the door, and I opened it to see Chief Langdon and Buddy. How did he get here so quickly? Wasn't he at home? He was, but as soon as we talked about my visit with Jake's father, he got in his car and came here. I'll bet he was missing his police cruiser with lights and sirens!

"Hi Mari," he said. "We need to talk." He glanced at the other people in the room, said a quick hello, and then he said, "Can we go somewhere private?"

Dad said, "You can have my office, if that works. We'll be in the family room. Is everything okay Chief?

"No, Ed. It's not," Chief snapped and turned toward me. He was glaring at me.

We moved into the kitchen and sat at the table. Dad stood in the doorway.

"Mari, I'm angry with you. And with good reason. Greg was in the area and you never let me know. Then he escaped, and now we may never see him again."

"I know, Chief. I was sort of stuck because I promised Jake I wouldn't tell."

"Sure, but this could have put you in danger. He could be the killer."

"Well, he's not. He said he wasn't, and I believed him." Now I was getting mad.

Dad moved out of the office, leaving me and the Chief to continue our argument. "Look, Chief, I've been working hard on this murder. She was my mother, and this has not been solved in fifteen years. Right now, I think I know who did it."

"Well, I'd feel more comfortable if I got to talk to Greg." He took out his phone and dialed. He waited for the ring, and I could hear a computer voice answer. Chief Langdon had an angry look on his face. He looked down and said, "The phone's been disconnected. I need to talk to him. Where does he live?"

"He lives about forty minutes from here. I met with him in a church office. "I gave him the name of the church and he went outside to call. He came back and was even angrier than before. "The secretary told me he just took off. He quit his job at the church and picked up his check on the way out of town."

"How could he do that?" I asked. "He had cattle to take care of. What will happen to them?"

"I don't know," Chief Langdon said. "All I know is that he left and they don't know where he went.

Great," he said, but he mumbled it under his breath, so I know it wasn't what he felt. I started to think this whole quest was a terrible idea. I'd hurt my grandparents' feelings, my dad's feelings, my friend Jake's feelings, and now, Chief Langdon was upset with me. What other disaster could I cause?

Chief Langdon said, "I want to look for Greg, but I don't think it'll do much good. But you and I should talk about what you found out." He pulled out a chair and sat down. Buddy sat near my feet, like he always did. He looked directly at me. "Start talking," Chief ordered.

Oh boy, he was right, although I didn't like the way he said it. We had to put everything together and show once and for all who the murderer was. I was getting close to solving this. I knew he wouldn't find Greg, but I didn't think it was going to matter. My brain was working overtime. I was frowning so hard my forehead hurt. And then I got a call from Emily. She needs to talk, not think here.

"Have you talked to Jake?" I asked.

"He still hasn't told his mother about Greg," she said.

"Keep me in the loop," I said, and went back to my conversation with Chief Langdon.

"OK, tell me what you're thinking. What have you got for me?"

"First, let me get Pupster." I ran upstairs to my room and found the plastic bag with Pupster that I had hidden in the back of my closet. I brought it back to the kitchen, and I also brought one of the matching hand towels.

"I can tell you who I think did it and why, thanks to Greg." I handed the bag to him.

He put the bag aside. "I'm listening."

"Do you remember my list of reasons why I thought somebody would commit murder? I've been back over that list, and it's helped me identify one person who I believe did it."

"And?"

"There were ten reasons if you remember, and out of those ten, I found six that fit the murderer's motive to kill my mother; revenge, anger, jealousy, hatred, to stop her from doing something, and crazy, although the last one is not for me to decide, so maybe there are only five."

"What are you basing this on?" The Chief took out a notepad and wrote what I was saying. "Do you have any hard evidence?"

"Not really, except for Pupster." And I told him my suspicions based on what Greg had told me and what I had found out on my own. "Even though my mother and Brenda were best friends and spent lots of time together, according to Greg, Mom had met some other friends through a book club in town and hung out with them and went to their meetings. You and I know this is true because of Mom's calendar with dates for the book club and the notes from the meetings, right?"

"Right," Chief Langdon said.

I went on, "Brenda became very jealous, and she got revenge for being left alone. She was jealous Mom had me, a girl, while Brenda had a boy. Although she didn't know the women in the book club, she hated them. Even though she wanted to get Mom to stop going to the book club, Mom refused. She invited Brenda, but she either couldn't or wouldn't go. When Mom came home and shared books from the group, it enraged Brenda even more. Finally, Brenda couldn't stand it anymore and killed my mother."

I paused to meet everyone's eyes. "She planned to do it after both Dad and Greg left for work, still very early in the morning before either Jake or I woke up. Because of her cleaning work, she had a white hazmat suit, which I remembered under hypnosis. She put on boots, but I think they had to be men's boots so she could slip them off easily, and she walked to the back entrance of 43 Windthorne, took off the boots, and went upstairs. he killed my mother and then came into my room just like I said in my hypnosis session, and she whispered, 'It's okay Sweetie. I'll be back.' Then she took the blue towel from the bathroom and cleaned up the blood on the floor and her suit and took the towel with her. Remember, she knows how to clean thoroughly because she's a professional. She went downstairs, put on the boots, and went out the back door and home to Jake. She must have taken a shower when she got home, wiped down the suit and put the towel in the washing machine. She knew she had all day to clean up before Dad or Greg came home. I wonder if she came back during the day to refill my Sippy cup or give me something to eat. She promised she'd be back."

Chief Langdon looked at me with wide eyes. "You might be right. This sounds very plausible. She was furious at your mother, it seems, so it would be a very violent crime. She could get to my house by walking behind her garage to the back door. There were bushes in between the houses, and no one would see her. We have a piece of towel belonging to your parents. Your mother's DNA from the blood would be on it, and it also was her towel. Maybe there could be some of Brenda's DNA on there, too. That would really help seal the deal. And I think you're right about the motive. You've done a great job! But I still need to follow up with my neighbor and see what he knows."

He stood up and picked up Buddy's leash and the plastic bag full of Pupster and walked toward the door. On the way, he leaned into the family room and said with a big smile on his face, "All right, Franklin family, I think this young woman solved Marianne's murder. I need to get back to Danbury, but I'll let you know what happens."

Chapter 50

I felt relieved, but also impatient waiting for Chief Langdon to call. Seth came over to hang out. Emily stopped by, and then Jodi and Nicole showed up. The crowd was together. We ordered a pizza and ate lots of Christmas cookies. Everybody was in an excellent mood, and I told them I was waiting for Chief Langdon to finish the investigation. We were close to the end of this horrible nightmare.

While we were all sitting in front of the fireplace, Emily got a call from Jake. She got up and went into the kitchen to take it, and when she came back, she told us that Chief Langdon asked Brenda to come to the police station for questioning. Seth looked at me.

"What's happening, Mari? Do you know?"

Emily told them how Jake's dad was alive and was living close to Rochester. I decided not to say any more.

"Let's just wait to see what the chief finds out, okay?" I said. "He'll call if there's anything to report."

A big conversation started among all my friends about what could be happening. What did Brenda know?

Jodi said, "We'll stay with you, Mari, until you hear from Chief Langdon. Em probably needs us too, so we'll be camping here until it's over." She got up and found Grandma and told her everyone was curled up on the couch and chairs in front of the fire. Finally, my phone rang. It was Chief Langdon.

"Mari, I talked to Phil Rowland and picked up the hazmat suit. He told me it had been tucked in among the stacks of trash at the curb. He never associated it with the murder until you talked with him. He likes to work around the house and thought he could use it. I'm having it tested for both your mother's and Brenda's DNA."

I turned to my friends and said, "I think it's over. Finally. We'll know soon."

Everyone sat there waiting for the final word from Chief Langdon. We went for a walk to clear our heads and get some fresh air. As soon as we got back to the house, my phone rang.

"We got the DNA results, Mari. You found the murderer. Brenda confessed a little while ago."

"Can I talk to her? I asked. "I need to finish this, Chief."

"She was processed and arraigned. But after she confessed, she told me over and over that she didn't want to hurt you. I'm with her now."

"Chief, she killed my mother- her best friend. That's enough pain for a lifetime. Like I said, I need to finish this for my mother and for me. I need to talk to her."

He put her on speaker, and I could feel my anger returning. My voice got loud as I yelled, "You are a murderer, sneaking into my house and taking an ax and killing my mother. You scared me, you broke my father's heart, and you lied about the murder for fifteen years. Why?"

Chief interrupted. "Your mother found new friends, and Brenda was jealous and angry, and that's why she killed her. I think you knew that."

"I'm angry too. She killed my mother, and then she tried to be my friend. How does somebody do that? How have you kept such a big secret for all these years? I hope she goes to prison for a long time, Chief." I felt tears running down my cheeks.

I looked around the room at all my friends. How would I feel if Em found a different friend? I think I'd be hurt, but I sure wouldn't kill her. And right now, we all needed to be there for her, for her boyfriend's sake. Jake's mother was sitting in jail and confessed to murder. What was he going to do?

Nicole said, "Mari, it's over. Your mom would be proud of your work in solving this case that went on for such a long time. Jake will work it out. I bet he'll find his dad again soon."

"Thank you for everything, Chief. Stay in touch." I hung up.

I stood up and went over to Emily and put my arms around her. Both of us were crying. I'm sure her heart was broken and she was worried about Jake. Then she moved away and said, "Mari, I need to go home and call Jake, but there's a surprise for you from Chief Langdon. You need to stay here. Seth will bring it over. Close your eyes."

In a few minutes Seth was back with a big object covered in black plastic bags. He put it in the center of the room and told me to take the plastic off. When I did, I cried even more. It was my mother's rocking chair and there was a note attached from Chief Langdon.

Hi Mari. This belongs to you. Chief Langdon.

Seth carried the rocking chair up to my room. It looked just like it belonged. He put his arms around me, kissed me and said, "Good job, Mari," and he winked at me. I brought out the blanket that belonged to the rocking chair, and I curled up in the chair with my journal. Seth covered me with the blanket and tucked it all around me. "I'll make sure everybody leaves and I'll see you tomorrow."

Then everything got quiet. My friends went home. I sat with the soft throw over me, just the way I imagined my mother put it over the both of us. Then I put my hand on her locket and wrote:

Dear Mom,

It's over. I worked so hard to find your killer, the person who took you away from me in such a terrible way. I hope you're resting more peacefully today knowing that we got her, and she's in jail. Chief Langdon was so committed, and he did an outstanding job of keeping us in his heart for all these years. He saved your chair. Grandma saved our throw. And what would we have done without Buddy the dog? My friends have stood with me through this, along with Dad and Grandma and Grandpa. I feel so loved by so many people, but especially by you. As your poem from Sonnet XLIII says, "I shall but love thee better after death."

Love, Mari.

When I finished the letter, I put away my journal, snuggled under my pink, blue and green baby blanket in my mother's rocking chair wearing her locket with XLIII engraved on the front, and fell asleep.

Chapter 51

A trial date was set for Brenda in Danbury. She was charged with murder in the first degree. Chief provided the District Attorney with all the evidence he had collected over the years, and the prosecutor made the case. We had to go to testify. Still, I would not have missed it. The four of us drove together to Connecticut, arriving the night before the trial and checking into a hotel so we could meet with the prosecutor and rest before our testimony. The next morning, we went to the courtroom. Brenda was brought in wearing a white blouse and black pants.

Grandma was called to testify about the monogrammed towels. The prosecutor showed her the ones we found in the attic.

"Mrs. Franklin, do you recognize these towels?

"Yes, I do." Grandma sat tall in the witness chair. She was dressed in her navy pantsuit looking very businesslike. "They came from my son's house. I packed them before he put the house on the market."

"Mrs. Franklin, is there anything unusual about this set of towels?"

"Yes, the set is monogrammed, and one of the monogrammed towels is missing."

I was not called to testify about what I had seen under hypnosis because that kind of testimony is not admissible in court, but I had to take the stand and testify about the towel that was used to stuff Buddy's dog toy.

"Ms. Franklin," asked the prosecutor, "where did the toy come from?"

"It was in a box in the basement of Brenda's house," I replied. "Seth gave it to Chief's dog Buddy, to play with and he left it in the back of my grandpa's car. Grandpa found it and gave it to me. When I went to repair the toy where Buddy had chewed it, I saw the monogram. Then I called Chief."

Mr. Rowland was called to the stand and was shown the white hazmat suit.

"Where did you get this, Mr. Rowland?" the Prosecutor asked.

"I found it in the trash pile in front of the Franklin house. I brought it home figuring I could use it someday."

The Medical Examiner was called to testify about the hazmat suit, how Brenda's DNA was found inside the white suit along with my mother's blood on the outside, all saved by Mr. Rowland, the snooper, who had picked through the trash and found the coveralls on trash day.

The jury deliberated for two days. They returned to present their verdict to the judge. Guilty!

Brenda looked at me with daggers in her eyes. Jake had tears in his. I turned to leave the courtroom and in the last row were Emily, Jodi, Nicole and of course, Seth–with those soft, blue eyes. My friends had tears in their eyes, too, as they ran to me and hugged me.

"It's over. Mari," said Jodi.

"We knew you'd solve it," Nicole smiled.

Emily came close and we both looked in each other's eyes. We didn't say a word. I knew how happy she was for me, but how sad she was for Jake.

I walked over to Jake who was sitting in the chair he had occupied all during the trial. I stood over him and put my hand on his shoulder.

"I'm so sorry for you, Jake. What will you do now?

He looked up and his face was blank. "I need to wait to hear my mother's sentence before I make any decisions. I have the house for now, college in the fall. I need to find my father. I'm sorry it turned out this way."

"I am, too."

Then Emily went over to him, took his hand, and kissed him. He stood up, put his arm around her and they walked out of the courtroom together.

Epilogue

One month later, we returned to the courtroom for the sentencing. The prosecutor told us that we could make a statement in front of the court. I planned to go and make a statement, but Dad, Grandma and Grandpa declined.

"You should do it, Mari." said Dad. "You worked hard to bring your mother's murderer to justice. "

I wrote my statement out in the notebook I used for my letters to my mother, and then I read it to the court.

"Your Honor,

My mother was brutally murdered. The murderer, Brenda Henderson, planned every second of it in advance and hid it for fourteen years. By her act, she cut short my childhood. She took away my mother. I missed her at every major life event I've had–14 birthdays, 14 Christmases, 14 Easters, 14 Mother's Days, helping me with my homework, shopping for clothes and countless school events. She will not be at my graduation. She will not help me buy a prom dress or send me off to college. When I met Brenda while trying to solve the murder, she saw how much I looked like my mother and clung to me the way I am sure she clung to her, with countless emails and invitations. Although she claimed to be, she was not my mother's friend at all. Nor is she mine. I want her to receive the maximum punishment for my mother's murder. I am afraid that if she goes free, I will be her next victim."

The judge looked at me, then at Brenda, and issued the maximum sentence. The guards walked her out of the courtroom, and the door closed with a thud and opened my life to new possibilities.

Acknowledgments

"Focus," they told me. "Keep writing," they said. I owe all of them so much for their help. My critique group: Rose O'Keefe, Marilee Waterstraat, and Valerie McPherson who read, re-read, and critiqued the story. My family, especially Jennifer, Hannah and Tessa McCarthy who helped with the YA perspective. Readers of the early draft: Jodi Incardona and Ellyn Chafitz. Thanks for your time, patience, and input.

The cover design was done by Kelly Artieri, who has done three of my picture books, each better than the last.

A special thanks goes to Douglas Nordquist, who, as a retired police chief, was an important resource and source of encouragement, information, and suggestions.

Also, Norine Passero, whose expertise with hypnosis contributed so much to the book.

And Dorothy Callahan, who provided excellent editing and many suggestions to help me provide clarity.

And my husband Bob, who gave me the time and encouragement I needed to make this book happen.

Thank you all!

JOANNE RUSSO INSULL

A former teacher and trainer who has worked with children and adults with disabilities, she has written and published five award-winning picture books and several short stories. Her children's books are stories about animals, and her published short stories, written for adults, range from horror to mystery to activism to surviving COVID. This is her first novel.

www.ingramcontent.com/pod-product-compliance
Ingram Content Group UK Ltd.
Pitfield, Milton Keynes, MK11 3LW, UK
UKHW012247290726
14090UKWH00013B/519